Pernickety BOO

First published in the United Kingdom by
HarperCollins *Children's Books* in 2024
HarperCollins *Children's Books* is a division of HarperCollins*Publishers* Ltd
1 London Bridge Street
London SE1 9GF

www.harpercollins.co.uk

HarperCollins*Publishers*
Macken House, 39/40 Mayor Street Upper
Dublin 1, D01 C9W8, Ireland

1

ISBN 978–0–00–860264–2

Sally Gardner and Chris Mould assert the moral right to be identified
as the author and illustrator of the work respectively.
A CIP catalogue record for this title is available from the British Library.

Typeset in font point size 11/leading 22 by Aldus LT Std
Printed and bound in the UK using 100% renewable electricity at CPI Group (UK) Ltd

Pernickety BOO

SALLY GARDNER

Illustrated by Chris Mould

HARPERCOLLINS
CHILDREN'S BOOKS

To the original Sylvie Moonshine,

my beloved granddaughter, Sylvie

CHAPTER

1

A sorcerer, finding himself caught in the rain, bought an umbrella – a non-folding, plain black stick umbrella. It was nothing out of the ordinary, and it might have stayed that way if it hadn't been bought by a sorcerer.

The sorcerer rushed home with it as fast as the wind and rain would let him. He'd just remembered he had left a spell on the boil, which was never a good idea. This particular spell came from *The Time Traveller's Book of Spells*, and the sorcerer was very excited when he saw it still bubbling away. The brew needed an urgent stir, but there was nothing handy to mix it with, except the umbrella.

It's only a cheap umbrella, he thought. But the second he put it in the cauldron it came to pieces and disappeared into the spell.

'Whoops,' said the sorcerer. 'But does it matter, I wonder?' And he went to look in *The Time Traveller's Book of Spells.*

10

At that moment, the doorbell rang. He had forgotten he'd invited his neighbour for tea. She had brought a sponge cake with raspberry jam and cream, and with her was Boo, her bouncy, hairy greyhound.

After they'd gone, the sorcerer went straight back to his spell. And so it was that cake crumbs and jam and dog hairs got muddled up in the mixture.

There was no sign of the umbrella. The sorcerer thought the spell was ruined.

'Oh bother,' he said, stamping his foot. 'Oh boohoo. It's gone wrong again.'

It was still raining the next morning, and the sorcerer was late for work in a magic shop near Embankment Station in London. He looked into the cauldron before he left, and to his surprise it was as clean as if brand-new. Resting by its side was the umbrella.

'Well, I never,' said the sorcerer. He picked the umbrella up without looking at it properly and rushed to catch an underground train on the Circle Line. At Embankment

Station, he jumped off, leaving the umbrella behind.

It went round and round and round the Circle Line all day. The only person who noticed it was a small boy.

'Hello,' said the umbrella.

'Gosh,' said the boy. The umbrella's handle was carved in the shape of a dog's head, with a very long snout and a shiny nose and ears that flopped back. 'You can talk.'

'I suppose I can,' said the umbrella.

'Do you have a name?' asked the boy.

'No,' said the umbrella. 'Do I need a name?'

'Yes,' said the small boy. 'You need one for someone to let you in at the front door, and another name to be let out of the back door.'

'Who are you talking to?' asked his mum.

'An umbrella,' said the boy.

'Don't be silly. Umbrellas can't talk,' she said.

And then they were gone.

Two ladies sat down, and the umbrella listened to them.

One lady said to her friend, 'You're so pernickety.'

PɛRNiɔkɛTy, thought the umbrella. What a

beautiful word. A magical word.

At Baker Street Station, the umbrella was handed in to the Lost Property Office, where it stayed for five years. The umbrella learned French, Spanish, German and Mandarin from other items of lost property.

At the end of five years, the umbrella knew who he was. He was Pernickety Boo, a well-educated umbrella with unexplored magical powers. And by then he knew what pernickety meant: finicky, finickety and particular. Which the umbrella thought described him perfectly.

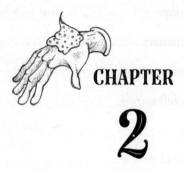

CHAPTER

2

Pernickety Boo made many friends at the Lost Property Office, especially among the umbrellas and walking sticks. As he was a sorcerer's umbrella, he was able to hop about and ask questions.

'Where do you come from?'

'How did you get here?'

He was disappointed to find so few of the lost items were given to talking. He had a great liking for the gloves, who never spoke a word. On grey days, he often found himself nibbling away at the fingers of a lost glove. No one ever came looking for lost gloves.

Pernickety Boo soon realised that lost property could be divided into three groups: the Long Lost, the Just Lost and the Truly Loved. The owners of the Truly Loved always came looking for them. Designer handbags, briefcases, watches, jewellery, even books fell into the Truly Loved group and so did quite a lot of toys.

Their owners would arrive in a flap and on spotting their Truly Loved would cry, 'Oh – thank goodness!'

And, 'I thought it was gone for good.'

And, 'I don't know what I would have done without it.'

And, 'Thank you very much for finding my bear.'

Hats and coats were nearly all Just Lost and were happy to see their wearers again, but the Long Lost sadly turned out to be mainly umbrellas and walking sticks of all shapes and sizes. Thousands of them were handed in to the Lost Property Office every year.

One day, Pernickety Boo found that if he took a deep breath and then opened his jaws, sparks flew out.

A bowed walking stick, amazed to find he now had a

voice, said, 'You need an owner – someone who will look after you and not leave you behind. Or,' he added sadly, 'lean on you too heavily.'

'Where do I find this owner? What does an owner look like?' asked Pernickety Boo, who wasn't too worried about being leaned on. After all, he could bend his head and touch his tips if needed.

'Usually,' said the bowed walking stick, 'they have two

legs and two arms and a round thing at the top called a head. It's good the round thing at the top is glued on to the body, otherwise they'd lose that too.'

Pernickety Boo hadn't come across any heads in the Lost Property Office, though he'd seen a few legs.

'A rubber ferrule on the bottom helps,' said the bowed walking stick gloomily. 'I don't have one.'

Pernickety Boo bent down to see if he had a rubber ferrule. He didn't, but he was beginning to have a fizzing, tingling feeling. It wasn't unpleasant. It made him feel special.

The walking stick was watching him. 'Aren't you worried you might snap in two when you do that?' he asked.

'No,' said Pernickety Boo. 'It's making me tingle. Perhaps it's because my owner was a sorcerer.'

'Maybe,' said the walking stick, 'maybe not. As I've never felt any tingling, I can't say.'

CHAPTER

3

'Fleetingly' was a word Pernickety Boo liked, and fleetingly he'd made friends with a designer handbag. To begin with, the handbag hadn't said a word. All Pernickety Boo could do was stare at her, admiring her beauty.

It was one afternoon when he had nothing better to do that he hopped up to her and took a deep breath. He breathed out, and again sparks flew from his jaws. The designer handbag jumped into the air. And then she started to speak.

It turned out his new friend was the most interesting of handbags.

'I will only be here fleetingly,' she said. 'I was soooooooo expensive, my owner will come for me at any moment.'

This turned out to be true.

'Here,' said the handbag, 'I have a postcard for you to remember me by.'

On the front was a picture of an odd-looking animal with a very long nose. Above it was a word: **Jumbo.**

'What does it mean?' asked Pernickety Boo.

'Jumbo?' said the designer handbag. 'It's a word for elephant.' And she vanished into the sunshine of a Truly Loved smile.

Pernickety Boo kept the postcard. He remembered the elephant and forgot the handbag. What was the point of clinging to the memory of something you'd never see again? What he needed was not a handbag friend but a brand-new owner, with a head firmly glued to its body.

One day, he heard that a collection of the most interesting umbrellas and walking sticks were to be taken to a Jumbo Sale at a place called Turnbury. Pernickety Boo knew that no umbrella was more interesting than him in the whole of the Lost Property Office.

Show me another well-educated umbrella, he thought. And I'm the only one who can breathe sparks.

A full-size mirror had been left on a train and handed in to the Lost Property Office, and so, for the first time, Pernickety Boo was able to take a look at himself.

He saw a most handsome umbrella. His canopy was a sombre black, but his handle was an elegant grey with just a hint of purple. He had a long snout with a shiny nose, sparkling eyes and a wide mouth that opened and shut. This was handy when he felt like speaking or nibbling a glove. Round his neck was a gleaming gold collar.

Yes, he thought, *an umbrella such as me belongs with a herd of elephants, not an owner with a wobbly head.*

He could see himself having tea with the elephants, going for walks with the elephants, shading the elephants from the sun, protecting them against the rain. He would be their all-weather friend, their one-and-only, never-to-be-lost-or-left-behind, best umbrella. Yes, things were going to be all right.

And with the postcard tucked neatly into his inner canopy, he went to sleep for what he hoped would be the last time on the green metal racks of the Lost Property Office.

All night he dreamed of elephants. In the morning, he felt as fresh as a newly rolled umbrella.

CHAPTER

4

Pernickety Boo had a big shock when he arrived at Turnbury Village Hall. There were no Jumbos – just a jumble of clothes and lots of things that could easily be found in the Lost Property Office. All of Pernickety Boo's dreams and hopes melted away. He had never felt blue before, not once in the five years at Baker Street. He had always seen the sunny side of life in the Lost Property Office.

At the Jumbo Sale, a woman tied a label to him, then put him in an umbrella stand with several other umbrellas – all of whom had nothing to say for themselves, nothing at all. Around him, tables were piled high with lost, unwanted objects. This sale was not what Pernickety Boo had imagined it would be.

When no one was looking, he hopped out of the umbrella stand, bent over and sat under a nearby table. Here Pernickety Boo had a good view of the legs of the people passing by. He hoped they had heads too, but if they did he couldn't see them. He knew he wouldn't like to be owned by any of the legs he saw. Perhaps he'd been better off at the Lost Property Office where at least he had lived in hope of one day being found.

He was wondering what to do next when a little girl wearing fairy wings and a clown hat crawled under the table and sat next to him. She was out of breath.

'Are you all right?' asked Pernickety Boo.

The little girl looked round to see who had spoken.

'Were you talking to me?' she said.

'Yes,' said Pernickety Boo. 'Hello.'

'I've never, ever, ever seen a talking umbrella before. Are you broken?' she asked.

'No,' said Pernickety Boo. 'Why?'

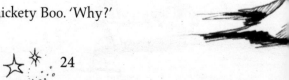

'You look as if you're broken,' said the little girl.

'I would have you know I can bend right down and stand up straight and hop about if needed,' said Pernickety Boo.

'Amazing,' said the little girl.

'And you look amazing. I've never seen a little girl close up,' said Pernickety Boo. 'Never, ever. Are you an owner?'

'What's that?'

'I'm trying to find out,' said Pernickety Boo. 'What are you doing under the table?'

The little girl straightened her clown hat and said, 'I thought I might be safe here. I'm hiding from Billy Turpin.' Pernickety Boo liked this little girl. She had blonde hair, a sweet face with a button nose and eyes the colour of the blue lino on the floor of the Lost Property Office.

'Billy Turpin is out to take my clown hat,' she explained with a sigh. 'He's a pain in the big toe.'

'Do you have a name?' asked Pernickety Boo.

'Of course I do. It's Sylvie Moonshine. Do you have a name?'

'I am Pernickety Boo, a well-educated umbrella from *The Time Traveller's Book of Spells*.'

'Georgie would love to meet you.'

'Who is Georgie?'

'A prop buyer some of the time and one of my mums all the time.'

'You have another mum?' asked Pernickety Boo.

'Yes, I have two. Georgie is a prop buyer, and Mum makes fairy wings.'

Pernickety Boo wanted to ask what a prop buyer was,

but this interesting conversation was rudely interrupted by the freckled face of a boy who squeezed himself under the table.

'You can't hide from me,' he said with a snarl, showing a big gap where his two front teeth should be.

'Now I'm for it,' said Sylvie Moonshine.

'Go away,' said Pernickety Boo.

'What did you say?' said Billy Turpin in a menacing kind of way.

Pernickety Boo didn't much like this boy. His face was wide and his eyes a little too close together.

'Go away,' repeated Pernickety Boo. 'Go away and bother someone else.'

'Wow – a talking umbrella! I don't want that silly clown hat,' said Billy Turpin, 'I want THIS.' And, without so much as a 'please' or a 'would you mind?', he tried to grab the umbrella.

'Leave Pernickety Boo alone,' said Sylvie Moonshine. 'He's not yours.'

'Not yours either,' said Billy. 'One pound fifty pence,'

he read from the label tied round Pernickety Boo's shiny gold collar. 'I'm going to get Dad, and he'll buy it for me. So there.'

Pernickety Boo was not the kind of umbrella to put up with being carelessly handled, especially not on a day when he had been bitterly disappointed about elephants. He'd waited five years to find an owner and had just met Sylvie Moonshine, an owner who was well worth waiting for. Sparks shot out of his mouth. They shimmered, then – with a POW! – headed straight for Billy Turpin.

Billy laughed. 'That's great! What else can it do?' And he snatched Pernickety Boo from Sylvie Moonshine's hands. 'Does it need batteries? Where do you put them?' he said, poking his finger into Pernickety Boo's mouth.

He crawled out from under the table, clutching Pernickety Boo, who slowly straightened himself up as Billy ran into the crowd.

'Dad, Dad!' he shouted. 'Look what I found!'

Billy's dad was a builder, and he lived next door to Sylvie Moonshine's granny.

Pernickety Boo wiggled round so he could see Sylvie Moonshine, who was now standing by the table. 'I'll be back!' he shouted to the little girl.

'No, you won't. You'll be mine,' said Billy Turpin. At the far end of the village hall was a huge man. 'Dad,' said Billy, 'buy me this umbrella. It talks and . . .'

Pernickety Boo took the deepest breath ever and showered Billy Turpin with sparks. Billy was so surprised he let go of Pernickety Boo, and his words were lost as he began to rise into the air.

Mr Turpin stared up at his son, who was now spinning on the ceiling fan. 'What are you doing? Stop playing about.'

'Get me down!' shouted Billy Turpin. He saw Pernickety Boo had hopped back over to Sylvie Moonshine.

'Hey, that's my umbrella,' said Billy Turpin as he spun round and round.

Sylvie Moonshine's two mums were watching.

'How did he get up there?' asked Georgie.

'He must have jumped,' said Mum. 'What an odd thing to do.'

'I'm not letting go of you again,' Sylvie Moonshine whispered to Pernickety Boo.

'Then buy me and I'm yours for keeps,' he said.

Sylvie Moonshine emptied out all the coins in her purse and showed them to the lady on the umbrella stall.

'Is that the right amount?' she asked.

But the lady was staring up at Billy Turpin. 'Yes, dear, yes,' she said, without looking at the coins.

Billy Turpin was spinning so fast that he flew off the ceiling fan and circled the village hall before crash-landing on the cake table.

'Once you've bought something, no one can take it away, can they?' said Sylvie Moonshine as she joined her mums.

'If they do,' said Georgie, 'it's called stealing.'

'Oh dear,' said Mum, looking at the cake table, 'what a mess. And poor Eleanor's lime and kiwi cake is ruined.'

'I can't take you anywhere,' said Mr Turpin, picking up his son. 'How many times have I told you not to climb up on things?'

'But I didn't! It was that umbrella,' said Billy Turpin.

'The next thing you'll be telling me is it can talk.'

'Shall we go home?' said Mum to Sylvie Moonshine.

CHAPTER

5

Outside the village hall, it was raining.

'It's been like this for ages,' said Mum. 'I'll be glad to see the sun again.'

'The car is some way away,' said Georgie. 'Do you think your umbrella might . . .'

Without another word being said, Pernickety Boo undid his popper and sprang open to his full glorious size. He hovered above Georgie. He had practised the hovering part when he thought he was going to a Jumbo Sale. He didn't know if an elephant could hold an umbrella.

Georgie and Mum were wonderstruck.

Sylvie Moonshine jumped up and down. 'Wow! Wow!' she said.

'I think you've bought the bargain of the year,' said Mum.

Pernickety Boo hovered helpfully above them until they reached the car. There he gave himself a good shake and closed his canopy. He twirled a few times until his folds were nice and neat, if a little wet. Then he bent over and popped his elastic tie into place with his mouth.

'Wait,' came a voice behind them. Billy Turpin, still covered in cake, marched up with his dad.

'See, Dad? See what the umbrella did?' said Billy. 'And it's mine.'

Safely in the car, Sylvie Moonshine held tight to Pernickety Boo.

'There's been a misunderstanding,' said Mr Turpin. He was a big man, and to Sylvie Moonshine he looked like a giant. 'I think that's my son's umbrella.'

'No, it isn't,' said Mum firmly. 'Sylvie Moonshine bought it fair and square with her pocket money. Good afternoon, Mr Turpin.'

 34

Mum climbed into the car and they set off, leaving Billy and his dad standing in the car park in the rain.

Well, thought Pernickety Boo, *at last I have an owner. Someone who rescues me from flying boys and red-faced Turpins; who holds on to me even when I'm soggy.*

'Where did you come from?' Mum asked as Georgie drove.

'*The Time Traveller's Book of Spells*. I was made in a cauldron,' said Pernickety Boo.

'Do you know the name of the person who made you?' asked Georgie.

'Nope,' said Pernickety Boo. 'He was a sorcerer with a wobbly head. He never came looking for me in all the five years I was at the Lost Property Office.'

'That's sad,' said Mum.

'Not really,' said Pernickety Boo, 'because now I have an owner whose head is firmly stuck on.'

Rain was running down the windows, and things outside were blurry. But he saw houses and trees, and people with dogs out walking. And lots of umbrellas.

Georgie said, 'Tell me about yourself, Pernickety Boo.'

'There's nothing much to tell, Mrs Moonshine.'

Sylvie Moonshine laughed. 'Georgie isn't a Mrs!'

'Call me Georgie,' said Georgie.

'And Mum Mum,' said Sylvie Moonshine.

'I lived for five years in the Lost Property Office in Baker Street. I speak French, Spanish, German and Mandarin. I'm an umbrella from *The Time Traveller's Book of Spells* and I have unexplored magical powers.'

Mum turned to look at Pernickety Boo. 'You can't really mean time travel, surely?'

'Why not?' said Georgie. 'A friend who works in special effects on films said she'd met a sorcerer who had tried to cast that spell. She told me he was very forgetful and couldn't remember if he'd succeeded or not.'

This conversation worried Pernickety Boo. Georgie couldn't be talking about the same sorcerer who had left him on the Circle Line, could she? A terrible thought crossed his mind. After all this time, he might have to go back to being a sorcerer's umbrella. He didn't want that – not now he'd found Sylvie Moonshine.

He thought it best to change the subject. 'To be frank, I'm not sure what I can do,' he said. 'Though I did talk to a designer handbag and a walking stick without a rubber ferrule.' He yawned.

'Nearly home now,' said Mum.

'Home,' repeated Pernickety Boo.

'What a magical word.

An **H** like a House,

an **O** as round as a hug,

an **M** for Mums

and an **E** for Ever.'

And almost before he'd finished speaking he'd fallen asleep with a distant memory of elephants.

Sylvie carried Pernickety Boo into the house, and he woke a little later to find he was in a small bed that Sylvie and Georgie had made for him. Next to his bed was a rather wet and soggy postcard of an elephant.

He lay with his eyes half closed, listening to Mum read bedtime stories to Sylvie Moonshine. They were from a book of fairy tales. He heard of a magic mirror and a wishing well.

Surely they should have their own book, he thought drowsily, not one cluttered with greedy queens and needy princesses.

Most importantly, both the magic mirror and the wishing well had something to say. Tucked up in his bed, it was good to know that he wasn't alone in being a non-human who could speak.

'Goodnight, Pernickety Boo,' said Sylvie Moonshine as Mum switched off the lamp. 'I'm so happy you found me.'

'So am I,' said Pernickety Boo. 'And may I never be lost again,' he added quietly to himself.

CHAPTER 6

Pernickety Boo woke early that first morning at Sylvie Moonshine's house. Umbrellas don't need as much sleep as humans, small or large. To pass the time, he took a tour round the bedroom. The walls were painted with elephants wearing hats, some walking on tightropes.

He realised that this day was a day of firsts. This was the first morning he had woken up in daylight. Daylight was lost at Baker Street. The building went down underground, not up towards the sky, and the noises he heard were of the tube trains rumbling along.

And this was the first time he'd seen so many things

that weren't lost all in one room. Sylvie Moonshine's toys were in boxes, and surprisingly none of them seemed to be awake or in the mood for talking.

Pernickety Boo looked at the book of fairy tales. He thought one day he would like to invite the wishing well and the magic mirror to have tea with him and Sylvie Moonshine.

At first he didn't notice the sunshine barging through the curtains and falling on the bedroom floor in a puddle of golden light. In the Lost Property Office at Baker Street there was never any sunshine – just a strip light that was switched on in the morning, crackled all day and was switched off at night.

Pernickety Boo knew what 'sunny' meant. He had seen sunshine in a smile, or so he believed. He had heard it said in the Lost Property Office that sunshine was golden, and here it was, in magical puddles. Why wasn't everyone awake, dancing in the garden, scooping up buckets of liquid gold to keep for when the lights went out?

When at last Sylvie Moonshine woke up, he tried to ask

her about the sunshine.
He hopped after her
to a small room
where she stood
on a little step
and brushed
her teeth.

'What's
that on the
brush?' asked
Pernickety Boo.

'Toothpaste,'
said Sylvie
Moonshine sleepily. 'I
brush my teeth when I wake
up. And before I go to bed.'

'And is that a wishing well?' he asked.

'No,' she said, giggling. 'It's a loo.'

Pernickety Boo was none the wiser.

'Shouldn't we catch the sunshine?' he asked.

'Yes, we should,' said Sylvie Moonshine. 'But I have to go to school.'

'What's school?'

'It's a place to learn things.'

'I could teach you things,' said Pernickety Boo. 'I know French and Mandarin. And then we would have time to catch the sun.'

Sylvie Moonshine yawned. 'Not today,' she said.

'Come on!' called Georgie from downstairs. 'Breakfast is on the table!'

'And I have a train to catch!' added Mum. 'Hurry, all of you!'

Pernickety Boo wondered if catching trains was the same as catching the sun. But before he could ask such a sensible question the house become a mass of whirling clothes and frantic mums. Pernickety Boo had no idea what was going on. At the Lost Property Office, no one rushed from here to there for no good reason.

Perhaps this is what you do when you're about to catch a train or catch the sun, he thought.

He hopped after Sylvie Moonshine as she rushed downstairs. He hopped after her as she rushed upstairs, and then back down again. He hopped after her as she and Mum and Georgie sat at the kitchen table. They had laid a place especially for Pernickety Boo.

'I don't know what you like to eat,' said Mum. 'There's freshly baked bread; there's butter and jam. I could do you an egg – or would you rather have cereal? Porridge, perhaps?'

He was hoping she might offer him gloves. When she didn't, Pernickety Boo thought it best to say, 'Nothing for me, thank you . . . er, Mum.'

There was, though, a glove at the end of the table. It looked delicious. He wondered what the fingers of the glove might taste like with jam. These happy thoughts were interrupted when everyone got up and started rushing around again.

'I can't take you to school with me, Pernickety Boo,' said

Sylvie Moonshine. 'Not today. I've got swimming.'

Swimming? thought Pernickety Boo. *Why go swimming?* He hopped after her. 'But what about catching the sun?'

Georgie opened the front door, and the sunshine poured into the hall. 'Come on, Sylvie Moonshine. I'll drive you to school and then take Mum to the station.'

'But the sun . . .' said Pernickety Boo.

'Yes, I know,' said Mum. 'It's shining. Makes a change. Have you got your swimming costume, Sylvie Moonshine?' She handed Sylvie Moonshine her lunch box. 'Okay – let's go.'

'Don't do anything until we come home,' said Georgie.

'Couldn't I just go out and catch the sun?' said Pernickety Boo.

'See you later, Pernickety Boo!' called Sylvie Moonshine.

'What about your fairy wings and your clown hat?' said Pernickety Boo.

But the front door had closed with a bang.

And all was quiet – a deep sort of quiet that only comes when everyone has left the house except for a time-travelling umbrella.

CHAPTER

7

Before leaving the Lost Property Office, Pernickety Boo had taken up morning exercises. First he had mastered hovering. Then he had thought that if a clock could boast hands, then surely he could use the tips of his ribs as fingers.

His exercises had been going well, and at Baker Street he became good at picking up handbags and briefcases, as they had handles. He had trouble with the fiddly things. The popper on the elastic tie that kept his canopy neatly furled was one that took some mastering.

With his new owner Sylvie Moonshine at school,

Pernickety Boo didn't know what to do with himself. The glove on the end of the breakfast table looked so tempting. It wouldn't matter, would it, if he just nibbled on a finger? He soon found it was the tastiest finger of any glove he had ever eaten. One finger led to another, then another and another, then a thumb.

Most gloves in the Lost Property Office were stale and a little too crispy. This glove was fresh and mouthwatering. Before Pernickety Boo could say, 'I love a good glove,' he found that he had eaten the whole thing.

Energy rushed through the core of him right to his tips. He thought about catching sunshine, but didn't know where to begin. Did he need a bucket? A fishing net? Then there was the problem of how to open the door. Surely he wasn't meant to stay as still as a statue all day? That wasn't his style. And what did Georgie mean when she said not to do anything until they came home? That didn't sound right.

Maybe he should throw himself into the day as Sylvie Moonshine and her mums had. After all, this was his first taste of freedom after five years at the Lost Property Office. He had a view of the outside world through the window. What could possibly go wrong for a particular, finicky, pernickety umbrella? The best thing he could do was to make the most of every moment.

He hopped back upstairs to have a word with the wishing well, or 'loo' as Sylvie called it. This was where the morning had begun, with Sylvie Moonshine brushing her teeth. Pernickety Boo wondered if he had teeth. He was disappointed to see there was no water in the duck pond – Sylvie Moonshine had called it a 'bath' – but there were a couple of pink plastic ducks waiting beside it.

The wishing well that Sylvie Moonshine called a loo had a lid. There was a roll of paper beside it; very useful for writing down wishes. Pernickety Boo lifted the lid.

'Hello!' he called. 'Is there anyone there?'

The wishing well refused to speak. Pernickety Boo spent some time trying to get a word out of it. He even tried breathing sparks at it, but it appeared to be a non-talking wishing well.

On the wall was a type of sink. Pernickety Boo recognised it from the taps. The cleaner at the Lost Property Office always got water from a tap. Here there were two taps, one marked C, the other marked H. Pernickety Boo hadn't a clue what C and H stood for. Above was a shelf on which were jars, bottles and odd-shaped tubes.

Magic potions, he thought.

A magic mirror hung on the wall, just like the one in the book of fairy tales.

Stretching out his canopy, Pernickety Boo put four of his tips on one side of the sink and four on the other. He pushed himself up onto the little step to look in the mirror. He remembered what the wicked queen had said in the fairy tale and thought he would give it a try.

'Mirror, mirror on the wall,' he said and leaned

forward to hear anything the mirror might say. He was pleased to see he had teeth.

'Well, I never imagined that,' he said to the mirror.

He managed to pick up a toothbrush and, with difficulty, take the cap off the tube of toothpaste. Try as he might, he couldn't get the toothpaste out of the tube.

Afterwards, he realised this was where things started to go a little wrong.

He put the tube of toothpaste on the floor and then hopped on it. The tube exploded, and toothpaste went everywhere.

'Whoops-a-daisy,' he said to himself.

He hopped back up onto the step to see if the magic mirror had something helpful to say, but the step slipped from under him.

Pernickety Boo was not slow to think fast. He quickly hooked himself onto the shelf, which wobbled alarmingly for a moment before crashing into the little sink, along with all the magic potions.

He could see this was quite bad, but it wasn't beyond

Pernickety Boo's ability to put everything right. Or so he thought. What happened next changed that. His tips were holding on to the sink that was now full of magic potions when suddenly it too came away from the wall. It swung back again, then forwards, then backwards, then forwards. Finally, it crashed to the floor. Most of the magic potions were thrown into the wishing well.

Somehow he had become hooked on a tap, and now he was certain the H on the top of the tap stood for Help.

His elastic tie was caught round the tap with the C on it, and there was water where he was certain water shouldn't be.

A house is nothing short of a disaster zone, thought Pernickety Boo. No wonder so many lost things enjoyed their stay at the Lost Property Office – they needed a well-earned rest from household calamities. Now he knew that C stood for Calamity.

'What to do?' he asked the wishing well, but it still stubbornly refused to say anything helpful. Perhaps it was upset at having the magic potions thrown down it without a 'hello' or a 'would you mind?' type of conversation beforehand.

Everything looked rather grim. To make matters worse, the sunshine had vanished. Now the room looked grey. Grim, grey and wet.

'Mirror, mirror on the wall, can you help me out at all?' said Pernickety Boo.

The mirror was silent. As was the bright pink duck floating on the floor.

How had it all gone so wrong? He'd only come in here

to see if he had teeth and to give them a good brush. Bits of glove were always getting stuck in his mouth. And all this was only supposed to take a minute. Now it looked as if he wouldn't be catching sunshine today at all, and he had a nasty feeling that no one would be best pleased to see the mess he'd made.

Pernickety Boo hopped out of the little room and onto the landing. He hoped if he closed the door it would magically put itself to rights. But then he accidentally hopped on another tube that squirted blue gunk everywhere. He found himself pirouetting then hurtling bumpety-bumpety-bump down to the foot of the stairs. He stood up and was relieved to find that none of his ribs were broken.

What to do? thought Pernickety Boo.

First he should clean up the mess. Then he must find the person in charge of the sunshine switch and ask him or her to turn the lights back on. The most worrying problem was HOW to clean up the little room. It was beyond him. He looked up the stairs to see the bright pink duck floating on the top step.

'Oh dear,' he said to the silent plastic bird. 'What will happen when Sylvie Moonshine and her mums return home and see the mess I've made?'

CHAPTER

8

It was worse than the fire drills at the Lost Property Office. Not that there ever was a fire – just much ringing of bells that jangled Pernickety Boo's canopy.

'I like order,' said Pernickety Boo aloud. 'And things in their place, not scattered about willy-nilly. And this house is so full of things that don't talk.' Forgetting about the bathroom for a moment, he hopped into the room he'd heard Georgie call the kitchen.

'Take this room. There are things everywhere, all jumbled together, like the room with the wishing well. It's most discombobulating.'

Saying 'discombobulating' was nearly as tasty in his mouth as nibbling a glove. He said it again. **'Discombobulating.'**

It was a comfort, but for a particular and finickity time-travelling Pernickety Boo this was no way to live.

Just then there was a flash of light outside. The person in charge of lights must be changing the sunshine bulb. There was a loud bang, and then it began to rain.

Pernickety Boo was looking out of the window at the rain and didn't see a cat with more fur than face slide in through a small door set in a bigger one.

The cat stopped, stared at Pernickety Boo and said, 'I saw you last night. You're new around here.'

'Oh, at last – someone who speaks.'

'My name is Jimjam. And you are?'

'I'm Pernickety Boo. A time-travelling umbrella.'

Jimjam loped into the hall, where the bright pink duck was threatening to slip down the stairs.

Pernickety Boo tried to explain as he followed him. 'I had a bit of trouble in the little room with the wishing well and the magic mirror,' he said.

'Mmm, you mean the bathroom,' said Jimjam. 'And what you're referring to is no wishing well. It's a toilet, you daft brolly. And, according to Georgie, that mirror has nothing good to say to anyone.'

Jimjam trotted up the stairs and quickly came down again, shaking the water from his paws. 'In all the years I've lived here at 3 Rose Terrace, I have never created such a mess.' He stopped, then said, 'Well, once I did a poopoo in Georgie's slipper, but I put that down to youthful folly.' He stared again at Pernickety Boo. 'Do you know you have the face of a dog?'

'I do. A greyhound,' said Pernickety Boo.

'Handsome, I give you that, but I don't much like dogs.'

Pernickety Boo leaned wearily against the wall and said, 'All I wanted was to find the person with the sunshine switch.'

'Don't we all,' said Jimjam, licking his chest.

Pernickety Boo sighed and accidentally breathed out a few sparks. To his surprise, the bright pink duck at the top of the stairs suddenly found her voice.

'We need a mop and a bucket – quickly.'

'The plastic duck has a point,' said Jimjam. 'And you have to turn the tap off.'

'I do?' said Pernickety Boo. 'But how? That tap has been waiting for a calamity. It has a C on it.'

'Cold,' said Jimjam. 'That's what C stands for.'

'Not Calamity?'

'No, the C is for Cold, the H for Hot.'

'Not Help?'

'No,' said Jimjam. 'Now, in that cupboard you'll find a mop and a bucket.'

Pernickety Boo breathed in deeply. Courage was what was needed. Maybe that's what the C on the tap really stood for. He breathed out a mighty shower of sparks. The cupboard door burst open, and there was a mop and a bucket.

'I work on a whirl system,' said the mop.

'Can you mop up the water in the bathroom?' asked Pernickety Boo.

'What is a mop for other than to mop up and keep a bucket company?' said the mop. 'Show me the way, soldier.'

'Actually, I'm a time-travelling umbrella,' said Pernickety Boo.

The mop, like him, could hop. And it began to hop cheerfully up the stairs, flicking its mophead as it went.

'He marched them up to the top of the hill,' sang the mop, 'and he marched them down again.'

Pernickety Boo carried the bucket and Jimjam followed them to the bathroom where he jumped onto the windowsill.

Pernickety Boo stood on the little step, unfolded his canopy, stretched his tips and twiddled the tap until the water stopped flowing. He felt himself to be full of Courage with a C.

The mop sang and whirled, and the whirling worked.

Emptying the bucket into the bath proved tricky, but the bright pink duck was a real help. As for the magic potions in the wishing well – that was a problem best left to hands.

Tidying took time. Pernickety Boo arranged the jars and tubes in a row on the floor in order of height. By the time they'd finished, the mop, the bucket, the bright pink duck, Jimjam and, most important of all, Pernickety Boo thought the room looked a lot better.

Just then they heard the front door open.

'I'm off,' muttered Jimjam and silently disappeared.

The bright pink plastic duck returned to the side of the bath. The mop stopped singing and stood to attention alongside the bucket. Which left Pernickety Boo alone to face whatever or whoever was coming up the stairs.

CHAPTER

9

Pernickety Boo hopped out of the bathroom and stood still as a man climbed upstairs, whistling. When the man reached the landing – which was wet – he stopped and scratched his bald head. Pernickety Boo saw he had a large nose in a round, smiling face.

'A slight misunderstanding with the shelf,' said Pernickety Boo.

'Rubber ducks!' said the man.

'Yes, that too,' said Pernickety Boo.

'No, no, I meant . . . I thought Georgie was joking when she said . . . ' – he looked at a piece of paper to see exactly what she had written – 'when she said not to be surprised by a talking umbrella.'

'I come from *The Time Traveller's Book of Spells*.'

'Yes, that's what she wrote,' said the man. 'I'm Fred Spinks, handyman. I often do bits and pieces round the house for Georgie. She leaves the key under the mat for me.'

Mr Spinks bent down to take a better look at Pernickety Boo. 'You're a very smart umbrella, if I may say so.'

'You may, Mr Spinks,' said Pernickety Boo and hopped back into the bathroom. 'Most of the potions . . .'

'Went down the toilet by the looks of things,' said Mr Spinks, 'but everything else is tidy enough. That basin was loose anyway. I wouldn't worry.'

'You wouldn't?' said Pernickety Boo. 'What a relief. You see, I've never lived in a house before. I'm used to the Lost Property Office, where everything has its place.'

'That's fine. Leave it to me.'

Mr Spinks bent to stroke Jimjam, who had reappeared as silently as he had disappeared.

'He always does this,' said Jimjam to Pernickety Boo. 'It's not unpleasant, and I like a little tickle now and again.'

'Nice kitty,' cooed Mr Spinks. 'Good kitty.'

'My name, for the hundredth time, is Jimjam.' The cat shook himself and stalked off.

'Do you understand what Jimjam is saying, Mr Spinks?' asked Pernickety Boo.

'Of course I don't,' said Mr Spinks, laughing. 'No one speaks Cat.'

Pernickety Boo went downstairs to the kitchen to see if the person in charge of the sunshine switch had had any luck changing the light bulb. But it was still raining.

He looked at the jumble of things and decided he would make a start at bringing order to the kitchen.

'All done and dusted!' called Mr Spinks from the hall. 'I disinfected the things that fell in the toilet and put them back on the shelf. Bye now.'

'Thank you, Mr Spinks!' called Pernickety Boo as the front door closed.

CHAPTER

10

Pernickety Boo felt full of life as he hopped round the kitchen. He would tidy everything away. At the Lost Property Office, things came in jumbled together and then were sorted into piles. Coats with coats, hats with hats, and so on. That's what he should do. Pile everything in the middle of the room and start at the beginning, sorting and then putting things away in their right place. Georgie, Mum and Sylvie Moonshine would be thrilled to see how helpful he'd been.

The pile of objects steadily grew. Three non-matching chairs, jars of herbs and jars of jam in various sizes, two kettles, teapots – too many to count, plates – lots, in different sizes, dishes, biscuit tins, a washing-up rack, cups and mugs, saucepans, cutlery and chopping boards. Pernickety Boo was disappointed not to find another glove to nibble on.

The pile took up most of the middle of the room. He was about to hop on the one chair that wasn't buried so he could take down the cuckoo clock when Jimjam, who had been asleep on the radiator, opened an eye. He jumped up, his fur standing on end.

'Whistling whiskers!' he said. 'What have you done now? You're nothing short of a hopping disaster zone.' He curled his long tail over his eyes, then looked again. 'This is a CATASTROPHE! Capital **C-A-T-A-S-T-R-O-P-H-E!**'

'I thought I'd sort everything out and tidy up,' said Pernickety Boo. 'In the Lost Property Office, they make an enormous pile and . . .'

'Oh no, no, no,' said Jimjam. 'This is a home, not a Lost Property Office. The kitchen is wrecked, you daft brolly. It's the worst mess I've ever seen – far worse than the bathroom.

'Mum and Georgie spend ages putting things where they want them to be.'

It was beginning to dawn on Pernickety Boo that he had made a big mistake. What happened in a home was different to what happened in the Baker Street Lost Property Office. And, when he thought about it, at the Lost Property Office, there were humans of different heights and sizes to put things away. Not just one umbrella.

Jimjam looked at the cuckoo clock and rushed about the kitchen. 'They'll be home in less than seven minutes. They won't be happy humans, I can tell you. You'll be put out for the bin men to collect. At best taken to the charity shop.'

'You mean . . . you mean they'll ask me to leave?'

'Ask? No, they won't ask. They'll want to see the back of you. And here was I just beginning to like you.'

Jimjam trotted to the front door. 'Yep, CATastrophic. I can hear Georgie's car coming down the road. Now you're for it. There's no time to try and help you. Not even one of my nine lives would get you out of this jam.'

And he returned to his place on the radiator and went back to sleep.

Pernickety Boo felt panicky in a way he never had at the Lost Property Office. He jumped up and down on the spot, his eyes tightly closed.

At first he didn't realise what was happening around him. But when he opened his eyes he saw the hands of the cuckoo clock had started to go backwards. Then the pile in the middle of the room became smaller and smaller until everything was returned to its place.

And Mr Spinks was standing in the hall, saying, 'All done and dusted! I disinfected the things that fell in the toilet and put them back on the shelf. Bye now.'

Pernickety Boo hopped after him as the front door closed. 'Thank you, Mr Spinks. And thank you again.'

He returned to the kitchen. No, he hadn't been seeing things. It was just as it had been before he decided to tidy up. What puzzled him was that somehow it looked cleaner and newer. As for Jimjam, he was still fast asleep on the radiator.

Pernickety Boo woke him up. 'It's all back to how it was,' he said.

Jimjam yawned. 'What's all back?'

He stretched, leaped off the radiator and slid through the small door into the garden.

It occurred to Pernickety Boo that he had just travelled in time.

Really, truly, travelled back in time.

Not by very much, but a little had made all the difference. He suddenly felt very tired and lay down on the spot and fell asleep.

 70

He was woken by the sound of the front door flying open. The kitchen was full of sunlight, and Sylvie Moonshine was calling his name.

'Pernickety Boo, where are you?' She ran into the kitchen, picked him up and twirled him round. 'Pernickety Boo,' she said, 'I've missed you. Have you been very bored without me?'

CHAPTER

11

Pernickety Boo was beginning to understand that school mornings at Sylvie Moonshine's home were always the same, involving things that could be easily forgotten or lost – her gym shoes, her lunch box, her coat – and there would always be a dash and a crash to leave the house on time.

When at last the family had left, Pernickety Boo, being a finickety sort of umbrella, would try to tidy up – just a little. He thought he was doing well – no major accidents, no problems with the plumbing – until one morning he hopped by mistake onto a roller skate and zoomed into something hard in the corner of the kitchen. He bashed his nose, fell to the floor and saw stars.

Jimjam trotted up to him. 'No ribs broken?' he asked. 'Nose all right?'

Pernickety Boo stood up and checked himself. 'I'm okay, thank you,' he said.

'That's my scratching board you came a cropper on,' said Jimjam.

'Scratching board?' repeated Pernickety Boo.

'Yes, I have to keep my claws in shape for my late-night wanderings,' said Jimjam, and scratched the object furiously.

To his surprise, the scratching board said crossly, 'I am a wooden horse!'

Jimjam leaped into the air, his fur on end, and landed on the other side of the kitchen.

'I am NOT a scratching board,' added the wooden horse.

Pernickety Boo was also surprised. 'This is the first object in the house that has talked without my blowing sparks at it,' he said.

'Not so,' said Jimjam. 'A firework display of sparks came from your jaws as you crashed into him.'

The wooden horse yawned, shook itself fully awake and

moved its head from side to side. 'Perhaps you could help me. I seem to have lost my jokes and riddles.'

'I beg your pardon?' said Pernickety Boo.

'You know, jokes,' said the wooden horse. 'Such as, "What did the teacher say when the horse walked into the classroom?"'

Jimjam and Pernickety Boo stared at it.

'I don't know,' said Pernickety Boo. 'What's a horse? And why would a horse go to school?'

'That's good,' said Jimjam. '"What's a horse?"'

'No, that's not the answer,' said the wooden horse.

'What is the answer?' asked Jimjam.

'I've forgotten,' said the wooden horse. 'But I have another one.'

'Another what?' asked Pernickety Boo.

'Another joke,' said the wooden horse. 'Jokes make people laugh and are a good way to make friends, or so I've been told.'

Now the wooden horse had found his voice, he didn't seem to want to stop talking. 'What do you call a horse that lives next-door?'

'I don't know,' said Pernickety Boo.

'Me neither,' said Jimjam.

'Neither do I,' said the wooden horse sadly.

'I think the wooden horse isn't at all well,' Pernickety Boo said quietly to Jimjam.

'I am an antique,' said the wooden horse. 'I've had about

twenty-five owners, and the last one left me in a garage for forty years. My wheels have buckled and rusted, my paint has lost its varnish and my mane has fallen out. I need a HORSEpital.'

'That's a joke too,' muttered Jimjam to Pernickety Boo.

Pernickety Boo was wondering why the wooden horse's owner would leave him in a garage for forty years. Five years at the Lost Property Office had been long enough.

'A question,' said the wooden horse.

'Yes?' said Pernickety Boo, who had a few of his own he wanted to ask.

'A man rode his horse to town on Friday. The next day, he rode back on Friday. How was this possible?'

'I don't know,' said Jimjam. 'I'm Jimjam, and I'm sorry for using you as a scratching board.'

'Don't worry,' said the wooden horse. 'I'm called Crackers, and once I knew the punchlines to the jokes and the answers to the riddles. Now I've forgotten them all except one: "A little horse." That's the answer, but I can't remember the question.'

Pernickety Boo was wondering what could be done to help poor Crackers when, to his relief, he heard the key in the front door.

'Only me,' said Mum. 'Just picking up the wooden horse. Silly of me – in the rush this morning, I forgot to take it with me to my workshop.'

And Crackers and Mum were gone.

Pernickety Boo decided not to think about the wooden horse's twenty-five owners any more. What was the point of worrying about something he didn't understand?

It being a rainy kind of week, Jimjam stretched out on the sofa and watched daytime TV while raindrops rolled down the French windows. The garden looked soggy and uninviting.

'I suppose,' said Pernickety Boo, 'the person in charge of the sunshine switch is still having problems changing the light bulb.'

'It's never-ending,' said Jimjam, 'until suddenly the weather's warmer, and the sunshine switch is never turned off.'

Jimjam's favourite daytime programme was the horse racing.

Pernickety Boo hopped up to the TV and looked at the back of it and under it and to each side of it.

'What are you doing?' asked Jimjam.

'I'm curious to know how those people got in there,' said Pernickety Boo.

'Just sit down and watch,' said Jimjam. 'The telly is like the sunshine switch – best not to ask.'

The highlight of the day was when Sylvie Moonshine came home from school, bursting in, calling, 'Pernickety Boo, I've missed you!'

Pernickety Boo would call back, 'Sylvie Moonshine, what shall we do?'

What they did was play all sorts of games. Mainly to do with dressing-up. Sylvie Moonshine dressed Pernickety Boo as a pirate, a wolf and a walrus. Pernickety Boo could identify with the wolf, but he had no idea what a walrus was. Sylvie had written a play based on Little Red Riding

Hood to perform for her granny on Saturday.

'What big teeth you have,' said Sylvie Moonshine.

'Do I?' said Pernickety Boo.

'No, that's what I say to you in the play. Remember? You are pretending to be Granny,' said Sylvie Moonshine.

'Oh. But you can see I'm a wolf, can't you?'

Pernickety Boo had a good point, and another happy afternoon passed while Sylvie Moonshine found a disguise for Pernickety-Boo-as-Wolf: a shower cap, an old princess wig and a pair of heart-shaped sunglasses.

Mum brought the wooden horse back from the workshop on Friday evening.

'You've done a lovely job,' said Georgie, who was making the tea.

'He looks much better,' said Mum. 'And I found all these jokes inside him. Listen: "What's black and white and eats like a horse?"'

'A zebra,' said Sylvie Moonshine. 'It's a very old joke.'

'Here's another: "Why did the pony have to gargle?"'

'Oh, a pony, wait,' said Pernickety Boo. 'Does it have something to do with horse?'

'Yes,' said Mum. ' 'Because it was . . .'

'. . . it was a little HOARSE' said Pernickety Boo.

'Very good! And another: "What do you call a horse that lives next-door?"'

'That's easy,' said Sylvie Moonshine.

'It is?' said Pernickety Boo.

'Yes. 'A NEIGHbour.' You know a horse goes "neigh"?'

He didn't, but he did now. 'Is there one about Friday?' he asked.

Mum looked through the jokes. 'Yes, here it is. "A man rode his horse to town on Friday. The next day, he rode back on Friday. How was this possible?"'

'I know,' said Georgie. 'The horse was called Friday.'

And Mum and Sylvie Moonshine clapped and shouted, 'Well done!'

That night, when Mum came to kiss Sylvie Moonshine goodnight, Pernickety Boo asked if they could keep the wooden horse as it looked so happy now.

'No,' said Mum, laughing as she turned off the lamp. 'Tomorrow it's going to an antique fair.'

'Sylvie Moonshine, what's an antique?' asked Pernickety Boo after Mum had left the room.

'Mum mends old things – as well as making fairy wings – and then she sells them. That's how she earns a living.'

'What does that mean – earns a living?' asked Pernickety Boo.

But Sylvie Moonshine was fast asleep.

Pernickety Boo was confused. He lay on his back, he lay on his side. He tossed and turned, but it was no good – he couldn't sleep. He hopped downstairs to the hall, where Crackers stood covered in bubble wrap.

Jimjam had just come in from his late-night

wanderings when he saw Pernickety Boo looking at the toy horse. 'No,' said Jimjam, 'don't start him talking again.'

'I'm confused,' said Pernickety Boo.

'That's nothing new, you daft brolly,' said Jimjam.

'Do you earn a living?' asked Pernickety Boo.

Jimjam thought for a moment. 'I do. I curl up and look sweet; I purr – which takes more energy than you would imagine. I cause allergies, sick up fur balls – that always goes down a treat. For my services, I demand a bed on the radiator and good-quality cat food.'

'Do you think a finickety time-travelling umbrella would be thought of as an antique? And what is an antique fair?'

Jimjam stretched and yawned. 'It's where you're heading, my dear old brolly.' And he put his paws over his eyes and went to sleep.

Crackers said quietly, 'Don't worry. You have a family.'

'What does that mean?'

But Crackers said nothing more.

No, thought Pernickety Boo as he hopped back to his

little bed. Surely Sylvie Moonshine would never want to sell him? Or would she? The thought of losing her made him feel ordinary – as if there was nothing special about him. Just another of the thousands of lost and abandoned umbrellas that were handed in every year at the Lost Property Office in Baker Street.

'Oh dear,' he whispered to himself, 'there's so much I don't understand.'

CHAPTER
12

Saturday was a day Pernickety Boo knew as a Skeleton Staff Day; that's what the whole weekend was at the Lost Property Office. Only once in the five years he was there did a real skeleton turn up, and it was claimed the next day by two student doctors, who were very pleased to see Old Bony again.

But Saturday at 3 Rose Terrace was different. It meant tea and toast in bed for Mum, and TV and cereal for Sylvie Moonshine. Meanwhile, Georgie filled the car with nearly all of the kitchen. Pernickety Boo watched from the window as she stowed Crackers in the boot.

'Where's it all going?' asked Pernickety Boo nervously when Georgie came back inside. He was wondering if this is what would happen to him one day if he made another mess of things.

'To the antique fair,' said Georgie.

Pernickety Boo hopped up to Sylvie Moonshine. 'Am I an antique?' he asked.

'No, you are my dear Pernickety Boo,' she said, taking another spoonful of cereal.

What a relief, thought Pernickety Boo. Now he'd be able to enjoy Saturday. 'Sat' suggested sitting, and he thought it would be a relaxing kind of day. But things took a worrying turn when the phone in the hall rang.

Georgie took the call, then came back into the kitchen to say Mr Turpin has asked if Sylvie Moonshine would like to go round to play with his son Billy that afternoon.

'No,' said Sylvie Moonshine. 'Last time, remember, Billy Turpin and his dad tried to take Pernickety Boo from me, and I bet they're planning to do the same again. That's why they've invited me.'

'I thought Billy was after your clown hat,' said Georgie.

'He was, and now he isn't,' said Sylvie Moonshine. 'So, no, I don't want to play with him.'

Georgie said, 'You know the problems Granny's had with Mr Turpin and all the building work he's been doing next-door. They had a bit of an argument, and it might make things easier for her if you play with Billy. You don't have to take Pernickety Boo – you could leave him here, or at Granny's cottage.'

'But I don't want . . .' Sylvie Moonshine sighed. 'Oh, all right. If I must.'

'Is that a good idea – leaving me behind?' said Pernickety Boo.

'I'm taking you to Granny's,' said Sylvie Moonshine. 'I can't do my play without you. And I promise I won't let anything happen to you,' she added reassuringly.

Pernickety Boo began to feel that perhaps things were all right. He wasn't an antique; he was Sylvie Moonshine's umbrella. He sat with her and watched a pink-haired prince on the TV making fairy cakes, whatever they were. He hopped back to the kitchen where Georgie was drinking a mug of coffee, looking out of the window at another rainy day.

'What do you do for a living?' he asked.

'I buy props for film sets,' said Georgie.

'What are props?' asked Pernickety Boo. He didn't know what film sets were either, but decided he'd save that one for another time.

'All the bits and pieces needed to make the films look real,' said Georgie. 'You know, like furniture, ornaments, cups and saucers, walking sticks . . .'

The list went on and on and included umbrellas.

Pernickety Boo was trying to make sense of this moving world of stuff. It seemed to him that humans had enough trouble remembering their heads, let alone all the things they had to buy. No wonder so much got lost. But he thought it best to change the subject.

'What has Mr Turpin got to do with Granny?' he asked.

'Mr Turpin bought the house next-door,' said Georgie. 'Then, without permission, he knocked it down and built

. . . well, you'll see for yourself. He also built Billy a huge treehouse in his garden.'

'And it's not as good as mine!' called Sylvie Moonshine as she ran upstairs to get dressed.

Pernickety Boo looked out at the garden. He couldn't see a house in the tree.

Finally, everyone was ready to leave. Sylvie Moonshine stood in the hall, wearing her clown hat and fairy wings and carrying a rucksack.

'What's in there?' asked Georgie.

'Everything for my play,' said Sylvie Moonshine.

Mum came wafting down the stairs. Pernickety Boo thought she looked lovely in a beautiful velvet coat, her hair tied up with a scarf.

'I thought you were going to sell that coat today,' said Georgie.

Hearing those few words, Pernickety Boo's fears returned. Was it that simple? One day, they might just decide to sell something? Something like a Pernickety Boo? He hopped up to Sylvie Moonshine, and she gave him a hug.

'Oh, Georgie,' said Mum, seeing the empty kitchen. 'You should have waited. I would have helped.'

'You always say that, Mum,' said Sylvie Moonshine, 'and Georgie always packs the car.'

That made both mums laugh.

It was a squeeze getting Sylvie Moonshine and Pernickety Boo into the car with the antiques, but fortunately Granny didn't live very far away.

To pass the time, Pernickety Boo told them about the little boy on the Circle Line whose mum said umbrellas don't talk.

'They don't usually,' said Georgie. 'That's what makes you unique.'

'And valuable,' added Mum.

'What do you mean?' asked Pernickety Boo.

'You're worth a lot of money,' said Mum.

Pernickety Boo didn't find this a very comforting thought. He was becoming more and more convinced that he was destined for the next antique fair. He doubted that Sylvie Moonshine could save him. She had made it clear she didn't want to play with Billy Turpin, and no one had listened to her. He tried to look on the sunny side of his thoughts, except it was still raining.

They turned into a narrow lane, and Pernickety Boo saw, high in a tree, that there was indeed a house. It was towering over Granny's little thatched cottage. Georgie pulled up outside.

'Hello!' shouted Billy Turpin, riding up on his bike. He stopped in front of Granny's gate in a not-altogether friendly way. 'You're coming to play with me this afternoon. My friend Simon the Snake is coming too.' He was staring at Pernickety Boo. 'Dad's built me a treehouse,' he added.

'Can I get past you, Billy?' said Mum.

Billy got back on his bike. 'Don't forget to bring the umbrella,' he said as he cycled off.

Seeing that Sylvie Moonshine looked miserable, Mum said, 'It's only for an hour, and you can leave Pernickety Boo with Granny. She'll look after him.'

Granny opened the front door and wrapped her arms round Sylvie Moonshine. 'And this must be Pernickety

Boo,' she said as she waved goodbye to Mum and Georgie.

Granny's cottage was neat and tidy, but a treasure trove of stuff, with pictures on the walls and interesting objects everywhere. Pernickety Boo especially liked the photos of Sylvie Moonshine when she was tiny.

The morning was still cloudy and rainy, and Sylvie Moonshine and Granny spent the time looking at fabrics and dress designs. This wasn't Pernickety Boo's thing. Sylvie Moonshine explained that Granny made her dressing-up clothes.

In her bedroom, Granny opened a drawer full of gloves, and the sight of them made Pernickety Boo feel as hungry as the wolf in Red Riding Hood. All he could think about was gloves. Wherever he looked, he saw gloves. He thought it might be possible he would faint from longing to nibble on one.

After lunch, the sun came out, which made a huge difference. Given the choice between rain or sun, Pernickety Boo would take the golden sunshine every time.

'I have to go now,' said Sylvie Moonshine sadly. She took off her fairy wings and clown hat. 'Pernickety Boo, will you look after these until I'm back?'

He watched from the window as Granny took Sylvie to Billy Turpin's house.

'Is she going to be all right?' asked Pernickety Boo when Granny returned.

'I think so,' said Granny. 'It's only for an hour. I'm just going to pop to the shops to buy a cake for tea. I'll be back in time to pick her up.'

Pernickety Boo was left alone in the cottage, in charge of the fairy wings and the clown hat.

He tried to do nothing. He lay on the sofa to have a snooze, but all he could think about was the drawer filled with gloves. What harm could there be in looking at them? A drawer of gloves needs to be properly appreciated. He hopped upstairs into Granny's bedroom, undid his popper and, stretching out his canopy, used his rib tips to open the drawer.

There were so many gloves – a feast in mouthwatering

colours. Pernickety Boo wondered if there was a more delicious smell than that of fresh, clean leather gloves. One pair called out to him. They were red and as soft as a plum. He held one of them, sniffed it, and found he'd eaten nearly all of it without noticing. Whoops.

That's the thing about gloves. One is never enough, and they were meant to come in twos. This was the best glove he'd ever nibbled. The other glove looked a little lost all by itself. Whoops. Perhaps it won't be missed, Pernickety Boo thought as he ate the last finger.

He was about to hop out of the bedroom when something downstairs went bang. A voice that wasn't Granny's and sounded a lot like Billy Turpin's said, 'I told you I knew where the old bat leaves the key. I can see everything from my treehouse.'

Billy Turpin wasn't alone. Another voice, higher, moanier and presumably that of Simon the Snake, said, 'We shouldn't be doing this. Think of the trouble if she comes back. Or if

your dad finds out what we're doing. All for a stupid umbrella.'

'It's not stupid,' said Billy. 'You wait and see. Anyway, Dad is watching the footie. Let's try upstairs.'

The chest of drawers with the gloves was by the door, and Pernickety Boo hid behind it as the two boys entered the room. He saw Simon the Snake had a thin face and large eyes. He was taller than his friend and seemed bored.

'You should've found out where the thing was before you chained Sylvie Moonshine up,' said Simon the Snake. CHAINED HER UP? Pernickety Boo was shocked. That's all wrong, he thought, with no right to it.

The boys were looking under the bed and, as quietly as he could, Pernickety Boo started down the stairs. But the house was old and the stairs creaked, and he was only halfway when he felt hot, sticky hands grab him.

'Got you!' said Billy Turpin. 'Come on, Simon – let's get out of here.'

CHAPTER

13

Do nothing and stay calm, thought Pernickety Boo. Though he wasn't feeling calm exactly.

'Looks just like a boring old umbrella,' said Simon the Snake.

Perfect, thought Pernickety Boo. His plan, such as it was, was working. So far.

'It isn't boring,' said Billy. 'It talks and hops and sparks come from its mouth, and it doesn't need a battery.'

Simon the Snake was unimpressed. 'It's not as good as my new camera. If it's such an amazing umbrella, why isn't it saying anything?'

'Sylvie Moonshine will have to tell us how to work it,' said Billy.

'Or perhaps it's just a boring old umbrella,' said Simon the Snake. 'Anyway, I don't think you should have chained her up.'

Most definitely not, thought Pernickety Boo.

As they went down the stairs and out of the back door into the garden, he could see over Billy's shoulder that there were muddy footprints everywhere. Granny wouldn't be happy about that.

Billy didn't bother to close Granny's back door, but hurried through the hole he'd made in the garden fence.

'I don't think we shut the door,' said Simon the Snake.

'It doesn't matter. The silly old bat won't notice.'

She will, thought Pernickety Boo.

Without moving, all he could see of the Turpins' garden was a ladder propped against a tree trunk and Billy's bike lying next to it on the grass. But he couldn't help himself. He looked up. He saw the tree was very tall, and the treehouse was very high up. And, of course, it was raining again.

'See that?' said Billy. 'It moved its head.'

'No, it didn't – it's an umbrella,' said Simon the Snake.

'Well, it did,' said Billy. 'Anyway, I'll go up and get Sylvie Moonshine to tell me how to work it. Here.' He handed Pernickety Boo to Simon the Snake. 'You stay here and don't let go of that umbrella.'

Pernickety Boo thought the treehouse wasn't a safe place for his beloved owner-to-be. Surely anyone could see it was far too high?

'It's a waste of time!' shouted Simon the Snake at Billy, who was climbing the ladder. 'And I don't want to be out here in the rain with a boring umbrella standing under your wobbly treehouse. I've had enough. I'm going inside to watch the footie with your dad.'

'No – wait!' called Billy. 'You'll see, honest you will. Come back!'

Too late. Simon the Snake had leaned Pernickety Boo against the ladder and was walking back to the house.

'Don't just leave it there!' shouted Billy. 'I'll have to come back down now!'

'What to do? What to do?' said Pernickety Boo to

himself. Whatever that was, there wasn't much time to do it.

He unpopped his popper and opened his canopy. Billy Turpin arrived at the foot of the ladder just as Pernickety Boo started to float upwards. Head down was not his favourite position as it was harder to see where he was going. But needs must. There was no time to waste – he had to rescue his beloved owner.

Simon the Snake turned round just in time to see Pernickety Boo rising into the air. This was worth a picture. *Click-whir-click* went his camera. Billy had managed to grab hold of Pernickety Boo, and found his feet were leaving the ground. Meanwhile, the glass door of Mr Turpin's massive new extension opened, and Mr Turpin appeared.

'Billy! What on earth is going on?' he shouted, seeing his son being carried upwards by an umbrella. 'And what have you done with the little Moonshine girl?'

Simon the Snake was still busy taking photos on his new camera. 'This is amazing,' he said.

'Billy, come down this instant!' bellowed Mr Turpin.

Pernickety Boo wasn't coming down, and Billy wasn't

letting go. Together they landed on the treehouse platform.

'Wow! Could you do that again?' asked Billy.

'No,' said Pernickety Boo, swiftly turning himself the right way up and folding his canopy. He hopped up to Sylvie Moonshine, who was chained to a post inside the treehouse. 'Are you all right?' he asked her.

'I knew you'd rescue me,' she said, 'so I just waited.'

'I only wanted to play with Pernickety Boo,' said Billy, 'but you wouldn't let me.'

'He's not a toy, Billy Turpin,' said Sylvie Moonshine. 'Now open this padlock.'

'Where's the key?' said Pernickety Boo.

Billy searched his pockets. 'I must have dropped it,' he said.

'Billy, don't make me tell you again,' came Mr Turpin's voice. 'Come down here right now and bring Sylvie Moonshine with you.'

'I can't, Dad,' whined Billy. 'I've lost the key.'

'What's a key got to do with it?' asked his dad.

Simon the Snake said helpfully, 'He chained Sylvie

Moonshine to a post with his bike chain, Mr Turpin.'

Mr Turpin went red with fury. 'I'm coming up!' he yelled.

Pernickety Boo knew someone had to take charge, just as the manager of the Lost Property Office did when there was a fire drill. If ever there was a moment for Pernickety Boo to take charge, it was now.

He didn't know if it would work, but he gently breathed sparks onto the padlock and, to his relief, it sprang open.

The wind had picked up, and the treehouse was swaying in an alarming manner. Pernickety Boo quickly opened his canopy and stood on his head again. 'Hold on tight to me, Sylvie Moonshine,' he said.

And they glided gently down through the windswept branches into Granny's garden.

Click-whir-click went Simon the Snake's camera.

Granny had returned home from the shops to find muddy footprints everywhere, the back door open and Pernickety Boo missing.

'Granny!' said Sylvie Moonshine, rushing into the kitchen.

'What's happened?' asked Granny, and Sylvie Moonshine told her how she'd been taken prisoner and chained up by Billy Turpin and Simon the Snake, and how Pernickety Boo had rescued her.

'This is worse than terrible,' said Granny.

Pernickety Boo liked the idea of something being worse than terrible.

'Come on,' said Granny.

'Where are we going?' asked Sylvie Moonshine.

'To see Mr Turpin,' said Granny.

Sylvie Moonshine, holding Pernickety Boo very tightly, followed Granny as she strode out of her front door and into Mr Turpin's garden by the side gate.

Billy was back on the ground, but his father was nowhere to be seen.

'Where's your dad, Billy?' asked Granny.

'Up there,' said Billy, pointing to the treehouse.

'What's he doing up there?' asked Granny.

Billy shrugged as if he hadn't a clue. Then, as an afterthought, he said, 'He's stuck.'

Granny shouted up to the treehouse. 'Excuse me, Mr Turpin? I'm the old bat from next-door. I've put up with weeks of noise and mess, and now today my granddaughter was held prisoner, chained up in that treehouse by your son.'

Suddenly the wind blew even harder, and the skies darkened. It began to pour with rain, and the sound of an alarming crack came from the treehouse.

Pernickety Boo turned upside down, opened his canopy and hovered over Granny and Sylvie Moonshine.

Simon the Snake said, 'Do you think Billy's dad and the treehouse will come crashing down, and the police and the ambulance will arrive and . . .'

'No,' said Granny firmly. 'You and Billy should go into the house out of the rain.'

'I think we'll watch,' said Simon the Snake. This was turning out to be a much more exciting afternoon than he'd imagined.

'Mr Turpin, it's not safe up there in this wind and rain!' called Granny. 'Come down!'

'I can't, I'm stuck,'
came the strangled reply.

'Should I call the fire
brigade?' said Granny.
'They're good at getting
cats down from trees.'

'Cats, not elephants,'
said Simon the Snake,
sniggering.

'Pernickety Boo, you
and Sylvie Moonshine stay
here,' said Granny, and she
sprinted down the garden
to the tree. 'Don't move,
Mr Turpin!' she called.
'I'll come and
help you.'

It didn't take Granny long to climb up the ladder and help Mr Turpin safely down. He stood at the foot of the tree as shaky as a jelly.

'Thank you,' he said. 'I would have been in a bit of a pickle without your help.'

'That treehouse is not safe,' said Granny.

'You're right,' said Mr Turpin. 'I'll take it down tomorrow.'

'No, Dad!' said Billy.

'Yes, son,' said Mr Turpin. 'Now listen, you shouldn't lock up a little girl with a bicycle chain. Say you're sorry to Sylvie Moonshine.'

Billy looked at his feet. 'Sorry,' he said.

'I'm afraid "sorry" is not quite good enough,' said Granny. 'Billy and Simon broke in to my house and left footprints all over my carpet.'

Mr Turpin, still shaky, was now deflated.

Granny took Mr Turpin, Billy and Simon the Snake back to her house. Sylvie Moonshine and Pernickety Boo skipped along behind them.

As Granny put the kettle on, Mr Turpin said, 'I would like it if you would call me Donald.'

'And please call me Josie,' said Granny.

While Donald drank his tea, Billy and Simon the Snake hoovered the carpets.

After they'd gone, Granny said, 'Now, Sylvie Moonshine, let's have our tea and cake, and then you and Pernickety Boo can perform your play for me.'

Simon the Snake smiled to himself as he cycled home that afternoon. *When these photos come out*, he thought, *everyone will know that Pernickety Boo isn't just a boring old umbrella.*

CHAPTER

14

Pernickety Boo decided it was time to explore his unexplored magic powers. And perhaps try a bit more time travelling – nothing too complicated. It was important to make sure he returned to just when he'd left. What he didn't want was to get lost in time. Should anyone have asked him what his greatest fear was – which no one did – he would have said finding himself in the Baker Street Lost Property Office again. If an umbrella had a heart, and Pernickety Boo was sure he did, then his would surely break if he was to lose Sylvie Moonshine.

The best place for this experiment, he decided, was the

garden. But there was an obstacle: how to get to it when he couldn't open the back door. He spent the whole of Monday pondering the problem.

On Tuesday, Georgie was off work doing something oily with a motorbike in the garage, and Mum was home too, sorting out an order for fairy wings upstairs. With both mums fully occupied, this, thought Pernickety Boo, would be the perfect opportunity to understand how the catflap worked. Jimjam came in and went out whenever he felt like it.

Pernickety Boo lay on the floor and tried to push his end tip through the catflap. The little door wouldn't budge. He tried again, headfirst. Hopeless. Blowing sparks on it had no effect either.

Just then Jimjam came through the catflap, carrying a mouse in his mouth.

'Why does it open for you and not for me?' asked Pernickety Boo.

'Because, my dear old brolly, I have the magic eye on me. Oh catnip,' said Jimjam as the mouse escaped and ran for a hole in the skirting. 'That's what happens when you talk with a mouse in your mouth – they tend to escape.'

He was now lying on the floor with one paw in the mousehole. 'Gone. Flea-fiddle-flea,' he said, sitting up and licking himself crossly. 'That mouse was to provide my morning's entertainment.'

'How does that work exactly?' asked Pernickety Boo.

'How?' said Jimjam. 'Sometimes I forget you're just an umbrella without a feline understanding of life.

'I play with the mouse; I tease it; and, when it's nearly at its wits' end, I allow it to think it has escaped. Then I POUNCE and gobble it up.'

Pernickety Boo was a little shocked. 'That sounds rather horrid,' he said.

'I'm a cat. That's what we do.'

Jimjam was in a sulk. He crouched under a chair, where he had a good view of the hole in the skirting. 'Don't worry – it won't escape me.'

'I want to be able to go through the catflap into the garden,' said Pernickety Boo.

'Then you need this,' said Jimjam.

Pernickety Boo bent down and examined the metal tag hanging from Jimjam's collar.

'I have three of them,' said Jimjam. 'The other two are buried in the garden. I lend them to special friends when they need a sleepover or just a place to shelter from the rain.'

'What does it do?'

'Opens the catflap.'

'Could I have one?' asked Pernickety Boo.

Jimjam was still guarding the mousehole.

'Maybe. But not now. Now all I can think about is that mouse.'

The doorbell rang, and Mum came down the stairs into the hall, calling to Georgie.

'Are you expecting a delivery?'

'Nope!' Georgie called back.

Pernickety Boo peeked into the hall as Mum opened the front door. Standing on the step was a prim-looking woman wearing a raincoat. She was holding an umbrella and carried a plastic folder under her arm. It was not the raincoat, the umbrella or the folder Pernickety Boo noticed; it was her gloves. They were red suede. He hadn't had a nibble of a glove since Saturday at Granny's, and the sight of them made Pernickety Boo realise how hungry he was.

'My name is Ada Moore,' said the prim lady, 'and I'm a reporter with the local paper, the *Turnbury Echo*. May I come in?'

'What's this about?' asked Mum.

'Your umbrella,' said Ada Moore, and took a notepad and pen from her pocket.

'I'm afraid we're rather busy,' said Mum, and she tried to close the door.

But Ada Moore was a determined woman, and she used her foot to jam it open.

Jimjam briefly looked up from the mousehole. 'I would recommend silence,' he muttered to Pernickety Boo. 'And no hopping about.'

Pernickety Boo straightened up and rested himself against the kitchen radiator as Ada Moore followed Mum into the kitchen. Mum, he noticed, had managed to get glitter on her face and in her hair.

'It won't take long,' Ada Moore said. 'Oh, what a charming room – so colourful. You have such a lovely collection of . . . of . . . things.' She let out a squeak. 'This is the magic umbrella!' She picked up Pernickety Boo. 'I recognise it from the photos.'

Georgie came into the kitchen by the back door. She was wearing a mucky boilersuit and, wiping her hands on an oily cloth, said firmly, 'Put that umbrella down, please.'

'Oh, I'm sorry. Of course, I'm sure it's a sensitive soul,' said Ada Moore, taking off her gloves and leaving them on the kitchen table.

'It's just a plain umbrella,' said Georgie. 'Nothing more.'

A smug smile crossed Ada Moore's face. 'I don't think you could call this "just a plain umbrella".' She pulled out a chair and sat down. 'I wouldn't mind a coffee.'

Georgie was about to say that she could go and get her coffee elsewhere when Ada Moore opened her folder and put it on the table. It showed a collection of photos of Billy Turpin being carried up to the treehouse by Pernickety Boo. Mum and Georgie glanced at each other.

'They were taken by –' Ada Moore checked her notebook, '–Simon the Snake.' She laughed. 'I thought I'd got that wrong, but the boy really is happy to be known as Simon the Snake. These photos were taken with his brand-new camera.'

Georgie had put Pernickety Boo out of Ada Moore's

reach, but he was near enough to the kitchen table for the gloves to fill his mind. All he could think about was those red suede gloves, just as Jimjam could only think about the mouse.

'As you can see from this series of photos,' said Ada Moore, 'Billy Turpin is going up, not down.'

The kettle whistled, and Mum made a cup of coffee.

'Black with two sugars, please,' said Ada Moore.

Pernickety Boo saw that a finger of one of the red gloves was hanging over the edge of the kitchen table. It was too tempting for words. Ada Moore pushed the gloves away to make room for her mug of coffee. Now they were even nearer to Pernickety Boo, and Ada Moore was too busy talking to notice that he had hopped close enough to nibble the finger.

But the sudden sight of Pernickety Boo's

greyhound head made her jump. Pernickety Boo toppled over onto her, just as an upright umbrella might if not carefully propped up in a hat stand.

Georgie quickly took hold of him. 'As you can see, Ms Moore,' she said, 'this is an ordinary stick umbrella. The photos were taken by a brand-new, modern camera, and it's perfectly possible—'

'I know what you're going to say – that Simon the Snake fiddled with the photos. We had them checked out, and he didn't,' said Ada Moore. She added, 'I hate snakes.'

'I shouldn't think snakes are very keen on you,' said Mum.

'Oh, a joke,' said Ada Moore. 'I do love a joke.'

Pernickety Boo wondered if she knew the one about a horse called Friday, but fortunately Georgie had her hand firmly round his jaws.

From under the chair by the mousehole, Jimjam could see something had to be done. He sprang up onto the kitchen table and stuck his nose close to Ada Moore's face.

'Oh, oh – could you take the cat off the table? It's

just that—' Ada Moore sneezed. 'It's just that I'm—' She sneezed and sneezed again, knocking the gloves to the floor.

Jimjam jumped down, and only Pernickety Boo saw what happened next.

'Ms Moore,' said Mum, picking up the gloves and putting them back on the table, 'it's an umbrella. It's nothing out of the ordinary except that it has a rather handsome handle shaped like a greyhound's head, and the jaws open and shut.'

'I don't believe you,' said Ada Moore. She sneezed again. 'I can assure you these photos haven't been fiddled with, and I can prove it.'

She stood up, sneezed and put on her gloves. She sneezed again and then stared at her hands, amazed to see that one of her gloves had a finger and thumb missing.

'How did that happen?' she asked.

Mum and Georgie hadn't a clue. 'How strange,' said Mum.

'Very odd,' said Georgie. 'Perhaps the cat—'

But then Ada Moore screamed.

'My glove has bitten me!' she cried.

Mum and Georgie gazed at her as she took off the glove. Out fell the mouse.

Jimjam darted towards it, but Mum shooed him into the garden while Georgie caught the mouse in a tea towel.

Ada Moore had had enough of 3 Rose Terrace. She collected her umbrella, plastic folder and notebook and pen, and hurried to the front door, leaving her gloves on the table.

Mum, Georgie and Pernickety Boo watched her go.

'This won't be the last time you hear from me!' called Ada Moore from the gate.

CHAPTER

15

On Wednesday, Jimjam dug up one of his magic eyes for Pernickety Boo. But it proved tricky for Pernickety Boo to hold it in his jaws, and he feared he might swallow it. 'What do you want it for?' Sylvie Moonshine asked, making a bow out of pink ribbon.

'So I can get through the catflap,' said Pernickety Boo. 'I want to see if I can time travel and I think it would be safer to try it outdoors.'

Sylvie had turned to the circus she was making from her collection of toys. 'Could I come with you?'

'If it works, yes,' said Pernickety Boo. 'Where would you like to go?'

'To a circus. One with a trapeze artist and a tightrope walker and a man who eats fire, and a lady who is sawn in half. And, of course, it must have a ringmaster in a tall hat who says "roll up, roll up".'

'Of course,' said Pernickety Boo. 'I'll do my best.'

When Sylvie Moonshine was at school the next day, Pernickety Boo lay on the kitchen floor and, headfirst, pushed against the catflap. Bingo bash, he was in the garden. He hadn't a clue what 'bingo bash' meant, but it was what Georgie said when things went well. And today was going well.

The sunlight had been switched on and, standing up, he saw flowers alight with colour. At the end of the garden stood a magnificent tree, its branches still bare.

'You got through my catflap all right then,' said Jimjam, strolling up to him. 'So tell me, my dear old brolly, how does this time-travel lark work?'

'What are those yellow flowers?' said Pernickety Boo. 'And what is that tree?'

'Mum calls the flowers daffs,' said Jimjam. 'And that old tree is a horse chestnut tree.'

'Horse chestnut?' said Pernickety Boo. 'Is that another of Crackers' jokes?'

'No, it's what the tree's actually called. A horse chestnut or a conker tree.'

'Daffs . . . conkers,' said Pernickety Boo. 'Oh, Jimjam, isn't being outdoors wonderful?'

'Don't get carried away,' said Jimjam, arching his back and stretching out his forelegs.

'I think I'll try it . . . here,' said Pernickety Boo. 'Under the conker tree. Could you stand back?'

'Don't tell me – I'm blocking your sunshine,' said Jimjam.

'No,' said Pernickety Boo. 'But I need a bit of space for my experiment.'

Jimjam leaped onto the garden wall.

'Here I go,' said Pernickety Boo.

He decided to jump on the spot twenty-one times. He got off to a good start, but then began to wonder if he was counting right. Was the first jump a whole jump or just half a jump? And while he was wondering he forgot if he'd jumped ten times or ten-and-a-half times. He jumped another ten times and hoped that made twenty-one. It was only when he finally stopped that he remembered he'd never been good at arithmetic.

He was about to tell Jimjam it hadn't worked when he saw that the horse chestnut tree had shrunk, and there was no Jimjam. And there were no other houses around Rose Terrace. In a flap, he jumped another twenty-one times. Now there was no Rose Terrace, no chestnut tree, and he was standing in the middle of a field. Not far away, a horse-drawn carriage sped along a country lane, and the sound of a horn blasted out.

Now Pernickety Boo saw that he was not alone. Also in the field was an angry-looking bull. The bull pawed at the ground, steam came from its nostrils, and it began to trot – then charge – towards Pernickety Boo.

'What to do? What to do?' said Pernickety Boo.

He started to jump, counting backwards. But he lost count of how many jumps and half-jumps he had taken.

He found himself in the kitchen. The kettle was whistling, Mum was making coffee and Ada Moore was saying, 'Black with two sugars, please.'

He'd travelled back to Tuesday.

He tried again and arrived to find Ada Moore screaming about the mouse. It was on his third attempt that he ended up in the garden again, under the horse chestnut tree.

Jimjam was on the garden wall, right where he'd been when Pernickety Boo began his experiment.

'What exactly are you supposed to be doing?' said Jimjam.

'I've done it,' said Pernickety Boo, leaning against the horse chestnut tree. He suddenly felt very tired.

'I don't mean to pop your bubble, but what have you done?' said Jimjam.

'Haven't I been gone ages?' asked Pernickety Boo.

'What are you talking about, you daft brolly?' said

Jimjam. 'There hasn't been time for you to go anywhere.' Bored, he yawned, stretched, then dropped off the wall into next-door's garden.

But Pernickety Boo felt rather pleased with himself.

'How is the time travelling going?' asked Sylvie Moonshine when she got home from school. She was setting out her circus toys again.

'Quite well, I think,' said Pernickety Boo. He decided not to mention the bull.

'You know what you're like?' said Sylvie Moonshine. 'A magic wand. A big magic wand.'

'What's that?' asked Pernickety Boo.

'Something with magical powers. Look, I'll show you. Imagine I'm a . . .'

'A sorcerer?' said Pernickety Boo helpfully.

'Yes, a sorcerer,' said Sylvie Moonshine, and she picked up Pernickety Boo and waved him over her circus as if he was a wand. 'Then I say something like . . .'

'Bingo bash?' suggested Pernickety Boo.

'Abracadabra,' said Sylvie Moonshine. 'And bingo bash.'

As soon as she said the words, they were both thrown to the floor.

Mum came running up the stairs to see what had happened.

'Georgie!' she called. 'Come and see this!'

'Tea's nearly—' said Georgie as she followed her. She stopped at the bedroom door.

Sylvie Moonshine's toy circus had come to life. The toy elephants were parading round the ring, the bear on the tightrope ran daintily from one washing-up bottle to the other. The lions in the cardboard box began to roar. 'Roll up, roll up!' shouted the doll on the drum.

'This is quite . . . magical,' said Mum with a nervous laugh.

The spell was broken when Jimjam trotted in. He pounced on the bear, turned over the lions' cardboard box, tossed the clowns around, then ran off with one in his mouth. 'Jimjam!' said Sylvie Moonshine and the mums together.

But now the little circus was just a collection of mismatched toys again.

'Pernickety Boo, do it again!' cried Sylvie Moonshine.

But Pernickety Boo lay down on his bed. Magic, he thought, is exhausting.

That night, when Sylvie Moonshine and Pernickety Boo were asleep, Jimjam overheard Georgie and Mum talking.

'Do you think it's wise for Sylvie Moonshine to have

an umbrella that's so powerful?' said Mum. 'We don't know what else Pernickety Boo can do.'

'Don't you think children need a bit of magic in their lives?' said Georgie.

'That's true,' said Mum, laughing. 'They do. And they need adventures. But I'm worried about that reporter . . .'

It was sunny again the next day, and Pernickety Boo went out in the garden, hopped seventeen times on the spot and found a time and place that he thought Sylvie Moonshine might like. Then, counting backwards, he jumped seventeen times and arrived back in the present.

The next question was how Sylvie Moonshine could travel with him.

'You didn't happen to come across Doris in your time travels, did you?' said Jimjam.

'Not unless she was an angry bull,' said Pernickety Boo.

'She had a show with cats,' said Jimjam.

'What do you mean – a show with cats?' asked Pernickety Boo.

Jimjam looked vague. 'It was in my circus days – an early one of my nine lives. I was the star act in Doris's show. Another life,' he said, gazing into the distance. 'By the way, Mum and Georgie were talking last night. They were worrying about . . . something.'

At that moment, Jimjam's ears twitched. He'd picked up that someone was in the garden.

'Cooee!' called Ada Moore. She looked as if she'd scrambled through a bush. 'I wonder if I could just have a word with Mr Pernickety Boo.'

In her hand, she had a water pistol. 'Keep away, cat,' she said, and squirted water at Jimjam.

In a panic, he clung to Pernickety Boo who, also in a panic, began jumping on the spot. When he stopped, he was relieved to find Jimjam was still with him and Ada Moore wasn't. But it was a little too dark to see where they were.

'This isn't the garden of 3 Rose Terrace,' said Jimjam.

'Cling to me again, and I'll take us back,' said Pernickety Boo.

But then the lights came up to reveal a man in a top hat standing on an upturned painted bucket. Pernickety Boo looked up to see the top of a red-and-white-striped tent. He looked down and saw a floor covered in sawdust. He looked

about and saw, seated all around, hundreds of people with smiling faces.

'Oh no,' said Jimjam. 'You haven't – you have. Flea-fiddle-flea. You've brought me back to the circus.'

The man in the top hat said, 'Ladies and gentlemen, we may not have lions or elephants, but we do have Doris and her Amazing Cats!'

'We've returned to my kitten days – but I'm no longer a kitten,' said Jimjam. 'Dear old brolly, you have to get us home.'

Suddenly a ginger-haired, white-faced man wearing a spotty costume and huge shoes came pedalling fast towards them on a tiny bicycle.

'Who's he?' asked Pernickety Boo.

'Rocco the clown,' said Jimjam. 'And he's no friend of mine.'

'Then shouldn't we get out of his way and sit down and watch the show?' suggested Pernickety Boo.

'That's not possible,' said Jimjam.

'Why not?' asked Pernickety Boo.

'Because I am the show. Or rather the show is what I did in an earlier life.'

'You said you were the star act,' said Pernickety Boo as Rocco went whizzing past, loudly ringing a bell.

'Just get us home,' said Jimjam. 'And don't dilly-dally or Doris—'

It was then that a woman in a pink sparkling costume entered the ring. With one elegant swoop, she picked up Jimjam and tickled him under the chin.

The man in the top hat shouted, 'Ladies and gentlemen, a round of applause, please, for Doris and her Amazing Cat, Jimjam!'

CHAPTER

16

The lights dimmed. Pernickety Boo looked this way and that, but he couldn't see Jimjam. Suddenly a beam of light shone on his friend, who now had a ruff round his neck where his flea collar should have been and a small clown hat on his head. Doris's pink sparkly costume had a cat tail, and she was wearing a cat mask with little furry ears.

Still holding Jimjam, with one hand she showed the audience a set of bars and hoops, little platforms of different heights and even a swing. What was it all for? Pernickety Boo hadn't a clue. He had never seen anything like it at the Lost Property Office. He did think Doris looked rather silly.

And everything she said started with 'meow'.

'Meow. Ladies and gentlemen,' she said. 'Meow. It is my great pleasure to introduce to you the one and only, truly splendiferous Jimjam the Amazing Cat. Meow!'

Jimjam knew the routine like the back of his paw. He walked with a swagger along a silver bar before jumping through several tinselled hoops to land perfectly back on the silver bar. He swung on a swing to great applause. He balanced a plate on his nose.

Pernickety Boo could see his heart wasn't really in it though. This belonged to another life, thought Pernickety Boo, rather like my other life at the Lost Property Office.

Things must move forwards, not backwards, and he had to get them home to 3 Rose Terrace. He hopped nearer to Jimjam. But he hadn't seen Rocco coming towards him on the bicycle, and, before he knew it, he felt a firm hand round his snout. Rocco was calling out, 'Custard pies, custard pies!'

Pernickety Boo found he was being shaken and his canopy opened without so much as a 'please' or a 'thank you'. Rocco held him high over his head, still crying, 'Custard pies! Anyone want a custard pie?'

With a tug, Pernickety Boo freed himself from the clown's grasp and floated quickly towards Doris and Jimjam. For reasons that were beyond the brain of a time-travelling umbrella, a beam of light followed him, and wherever he went Rocco cycled after him as fast as he could, trying to catch him. All this was greeted with hoots of laughter from the audience.

Doris was none too pleased to see that an umbrella and

 136

a clown had upstaged her act, and she too tried to catch Pernickety Boo.

The ringmaster addressed the audience. 'Doris is having a little problem with Rocco the clown,' he said, treating it as a joke.

Rocco aimed a custard pie at Pernickety Boo, who dodged it, and it landed smack bang on Doris's cat mask.

Under her mask, Doris's face was red. She strode over to Rocco the clown, picked up one of his custard pies and slammed it into his white face.

Pernickety Boo saw his opportunity and floated speedily over to Jimjam, who was still balancing a plate on his nose.

'Time to leave,' said Pernickety Boo. But Jimjam was dazed. 'Time to go home to 3 Rose Terrace!' shouted Pernickety Boo above the cheers of the audience.

'Flea-fiddle-flea,' said Jimjam as a custard pie whizzed past his whiskers. 'Why did you bring me here, you daft brolly?' He jumped into Pernickety Boo's canopy and clung on to his ribs. 'This is one of my nine lives I would rather not revisit.'

As Pernickety Boo rose higher, the beam of light followed them. Jimjam shook off his hat and scratched at his ruff.

'Where to?' asked Pernickety Boo.

'Up to that platform,' said Jimjam, still scrabbling at the ruff.

'Is that the way out?' asked Pernickety Boo.

138

'No. But we can think what to do once we're up there.'

The beam of light was still on them, and they were now high up in the top of the red-and-white-striped circus tent.

Jimjam said, 'We're where the trapeze artists perform.' He looked down at the crowd. 'This was my life,' he said. 'Or one of them.'

Pernickety Boo saw a man and a lady on another platform, both in sparkly tights. The lady leaped onto a swing and seemed to be coming straight for them.

'The last time this happened, it didn't end well,' said Jimjam.

'Was I here then?' asked Pernickety Boo.

'No,' said Jimjam. 'At this point, my dear old brolly, I feel I should warn you I've used up most of my nine lives. So, unless you have a good idea for getting us back to my happy home, we're stuck here for good.'

'I do have a good idea,' said Pernickety Boo.

'A talking umbrella,' said the lady trapeze artist swinging elegantly past them.

The man trapeze artist zipped by them and, as the swings

crossed, the lady said, 'We should catch Doris's cat
and take him down. Come here, puddy-puddy.'

'No one calls me "puddy-puddy",' snarled Jimjam.

'How is the umbrella hovering like that?' asked the man
trapeze artist.

'Don't let Jimjam fall!' came a cry. It
was Doris, climbing up a ladder towards them.
'Hold tight,' said Pernickety Boo, and jumped. Down they
went towards the circus ring. 'When we land, don't let go.'
Doris was now on her way down the ladder, and Rocco the

clown was cycling round in circles, hoping to grab Pernickety Boo before he reached the ground.

Pernickety Boo went up again, then nearly came down again, then there was a lot more going up and coming down until finally he and Jimjam landed just before the clown reached them. Pernickety Boo closed his eyes, hopped on the spot and counted backwards.

He heard someone shout, 'NO!', there was a flash of light, and they were back in the garden at 3 Rose Terrace.

'Keep away, cat,' said Ada Moore, pointing the water pistol at Jimjam and squirting him.

But just then Georgie appeared. She was holding the garden hose.

'Ada Moore!' she shouted. 'What are you doing here? This is private property. You have no right to come into this garden, trying to steal our little girl's umbrella and frightening our cat with a water pistol. I call that cruelty to animals.'

'That cat wasn't wearing a ruff when I arrived,' said Ada Moore.

 142

'And no umbrella I know of can hop or stand up on its own. And I heard it talking.'

'Out now,' said Georgie.

'You don't know what you have, that's your trouble,' said Ada Moore.

'Oh, I do,' said Georgie. 'I have a garden hose.'

She twisted the nozzle and water spurted out. Georgie's aim was good.

'Oh, oh, oh!' Ada Moore shrieked as she tried to avoid the jet of water from the hose.

'And your trouble, Ms Moore, is you don't know when it's time to leave. Out,' Georgie repeated, 'NOW.'

Pernickety Boo and Jimjam watched Georgie escort the dripping-wet Ada Moore to the garden gate.

'This time-travel lark is not for cats,' said Jimjam. 'I don't want to do it again. I belong here and now, not back in one of my other lives.' He stalked off, then returned to where Pernickety Boo was still standing under the tree. 'And another thing. I don't want you telling anyone that I was once one of Doris's Amazing Cats.'

And with that he disappeared through the catflap into the kitchen for a good long sleep.

Georgie bolted the gate and came back. She looked curiously at Pernickety Boo. 'Where did Jimjam find the ruff?' she asked.

'In a circus,' said Pernickety Boo.

Georgie laughed. 'Of course he did,' she said.

Pernickety Boo followed her into the house and hopped upstairs for a lie-down. Like Jimjam, he was exhausted. Time travelling, he thought, wasn't as simple as hopping back to the past. It was full of near misses. And custard pies.

CHAPTER

17

After supper, they all played a guessing game. You had a card with a picture on one side that you weren't to show the other players and they had to guess what you were by asking you questions. Pernickety Boo found it great fun. He guessed everything: cat, clown, horse, handbag, umbrella.

Mum and Georgie thought it was funny and laughed a lot, but not Sylvie Moonshine. When she and Pernickety Boo were tucked up in their beds that night, she said it wasn't much of a game because no one else got a look-in.

'Oh,' said Pernickety Boo. 'Is that what's supposed to happen?'

'Yes, you're meant to let other people have a turn,' said Sylvie Moonshine.

Pernickety Boo sat up. 'But there were no other people,' he said. 'Only you and Mum and Georgie. Was I missing something?'

Sylvie Moonshine giggled. 'It doesn't matter, Pernickety Boo,' she said.

But he thought perhaps it did.

'Did you and Jimjam go time travelling?' asked Sylvie Moonshine, yawning.

Pernickety Boo had promised Jimjam he wouldn't say a word, so he yawned too, which wasn't the most comfortable thing for an umbrella to do, and went to sleep.

It was Saturday, and Pernickety Boo had begun to understand that the weekend didn't have the order that belonged to Monday to Friday. Saturdays were a bit like the guessing game – you never knew quite what was going to happen.

This Saturday, the person in charge of the sunshine switch turned it on to maximum strength, and the garden looked magical. Pernickety Boo wondered why there was ever any need to turn the switch off when every day could be this bright and cheerful. At breakfast, Mum said there was to be a lunch party for her and Georgie's friends.

'Sylvie Moonshine, would you play in the garden with Pernickety Boo while we get everything ready?' said Mum.

'Couldn't I watch cartoons?' said Sylvie Moonshine.

'It would be helpful if you went outside to play,' said Georgie.

Sylvie Moonshine was about to say, 'Do I have to?', but Pernickety Boo whispered, 'Shall we go time travelling?'

Mum and Georgie couldn't think what had come over Sylvie Moonshine when she rushed up to her bedroom.

Pernickety Boo followed her. 'You have to look as if you fit in,' he said.

'Yes, but fit in where? And when?' asked Sylvie Moonshine. 'Will there be elephants?'

Pernickety Boo wanted to surprise her. He studied her

147

princess costumes and chose one, and Sylvie Moonshine wore it with red spotty wellington boots, her clown hat and fairy wings.

Georgie took a photo of them both as they went into the garden.

'Now what?' asked Sylvie Moonshine when they were standing under the horse chestnut tree.

But Pernickety Boo hadn't thought about how they were going to jump together. It had been easy with Jimjam, who had clung to him. But Sylvie Moonshine was too big to cling, and what would happen if she jumped fewer or more times than he did? The last thing he wanted was for them to find themselves with Doris and her Amazing Cats or, for that matter, anywhere he hadn't already explored.

He explained that seventeen was the number of jumps, and it couldn't be less and it mustn't be more.

'Otherwise I might lose you,' said Sylvie Moonshine.

That he might be lost or might lose Sylvie Moonshine hadn't crossed Pernickety Boo's mind until now. And, on the brink of an adventure, he wondered if it was such a good idea.

Mum came into the garden with biscuits and orange juice. 'What are you playing?' she asked.

'We're going to try to time travel,' said Pernickety Boo.

For a moment, Mum looked a little anxious, but then Georgie called, 'Rosemary!' from the kitchen window.

'Coming!' said Mum. 'Now don't time travel too far. Remember to be back for lunch.' She cut a sprig of rosemary and went into the kitchen.

Sylvie Moonshine ate a biscuit while Pernickety Boo wished there was a glove to nibble on. He always thought better when he had one to chew.

'Let's try this,' he said after a while. 'Put your feet round my end tip and hold on to my collar. Let me do the jumping. Ready?'

'Yes!' said Sylvie Moonshine, and her 'Yes!' had a spring in it.

'Close your eyes,' said Pernickety Boo. A tingle went through him as he started to jump on the spot.

149

After seventeen jumps, he said, 'Now open your eyes.'

'It's the seaside!' said Sylvie Moonshine as she looked out over the railings of the promenade, down to the sandy beach with the sea beyond. 'Wow, wow, Pernickety Boo, you did it!'

It wasn't anything like the beach Sylvie Moonshine

had been to with her mums. This one was much busier, and there were donkey rides and a red-and-white-striped puppet theatre. Watching the puppet show was a little girl of about Sylvie's age, wearing a pretty white lace dress and a big bow in her hair. Sunlight glimmered on the water.

'Look, Pernickety Boo,' said Sylvie Moonshine, pointing to the funny huts on wheels that were sitting in the sea.

'What are they for?' asked Pernickety Boo.

As they watched, out of one came a lady wearing a frilly cap and a short dress over long knickers.

'I suppose she doesn't want to be seen until she's in the sea,' said Sylvie Moonshine. 'I think this must be a very long time ago.'

'Seventeen hops,' said Pernickety Boo.

They turned at the sound of a brass band, and Sylvie Moonshine saw a parade coming towards them led by people carrying a huge banner that read "The Annual Umbrella Parade."

'An umbrella parade,' said Pernickety Boo. 'You see – once we were loved and not forgotten on underground trains.'

'You're still loved,' said Sylvie Moonshine. 'You're my best friend in all the world and back to here.' She thought for a moment. 'Wherever here is.'

Pernickety Boo was taking in the wondrous sight of so many umbrellas of all sizes and colours – parasols, paper umbrellas, wax umbrellas, sunshades – all being held high in the air. He longed to be among them.

'I bet there's not another one here from *The Time Traveller's Book of Spells*,' said Sylvie Moonshine.

Pernickety Boo left her side for only a moment and hopped nearer to the parade to have a better look – and just then he felt a strong hand take hold of him.

'My umbrella,' said a gentleman in a straw boater. 'I've been looking everywhere for it.'

Panic came over Pernickety Boo as he found himself separated from Sylvie Moonshine. *What to do? What to do?*

'What shall I do, Pernickety Boo?' cried Sylvie Moonshine, running to keep up as the gentleman in the straw boater marched to the head of the procession. He stopped when he came to a small raised platform that was decorated with bunting. He climbed the steps and addressed the crowd.

'Ladies and gentlemen,' he said. 'At this, the Umbrella Society's annual parade, when we celebrate the joys of the umbrella, I'm pleased to announce that I have at long last found my own umbrella.'

Pernickety Boo was sure he'd never seen this man before.

'Excuse me,' he said, 'I think you've made a mistake.'

The gentleman in the straw boater wasn't listening.

He took off his gloves and accidentally put them in Pernickety Boo's mouth.

They were white kid and very tasty, and in two bites they were gone. Pernickety Boo had often noticed that after eating an expensive glove he was full of boundless energy. The gentleman leaned Pernickety Boo against the wooden rail while he gave his speech. This was Pernickety Boo's chance to make his escape, but the gentleman caught hold of him again.

'Where are my gloves?' he said, looking to see if he'd dropped them.

'I ate them,' said Pernickety Boo boldly.

The people in the parade had come with their umbrellas to listen to their chairman make his speech, and they began to laugh.

'So amusing,' said a lady.

But the gentleman in the straw boater didn't think it was at all amusing, which made everyone laugh all the more.

Sylvie Moonshine said, 'Excuse me,' and, 'May I get past, please?' until she reached the platform. She clambered up onto it and said to the gentleman, 'That's my umbrella.'

'Go away, little girl,' he said. 'We will be judging the fancy-dress competition later.'

'No, that's my umbrella,' said Sylvie Moonshine. 'You took it from me.'

'This can't possibly be your umbrella,' said the gentleman. 'It is far too big for a little girl. It's mine – you can see it is.'

'You can't just go around taking other people's umbrellas because you think they're the wrong size,' said Sylvie Moonshine. 'That's stealing.'

This was Pernickety Boo's moment. He let out a bark of sparks, and in an instant all the umbrellas, parasols and sunshades 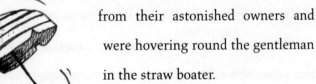 freed themselves

 from their astonished owners and were hovering round the gentleman in the straw boater.

The brass band stopped playing.

'Now listen here, little girl,' said

the gentleman, looking nervously at the umbrellas that seemed to be hanging over him in a threatening kind of way, 'as I said, this umbrella is far too big for you.'

'What do you mean?' said Sylvie Moonshine innocently.

The crowd was quiet as the gentleman in the straw boater took hold of Pernickety Boo and opened his canopy.

'You see,' he said to the crowd, 'this umbrella is for a gentleman, not a child. They are the wrong size for each other.'

Being upside down and with the gentleman's hand over his snout, it wasn't easy for Pernickety Boo to see what was going on.

'Let me show you,' said Sylvie Moonshine.

The crowd shouted, 'Yes, let her show you!'

'Very well,' said the gentleman, sounding nearly as grumpy as Sylvie Moonshine had when Pernickety Boo had won the guessing game. 'But this umbrella is mine.'

He handed Pernickety Boo to Sylvie Moonshine.

The second Sylvie Moonshine had both her hands round Pernickety Boo's collar, Pernickety Boo said, 'Hold tight,' and they floated high above the crowd, followed by all the other umbrellas and parasols. In the bright sunshine, they looked like a flock of colourful birds taking to the sky.

'Well done, Sylvie Moonshine,' said Pernickety Boo as they landed behind a fisherman's hut. He quickly turned handle-up and rolled himself neatly. Sylvie Moonshine put her feet either side of his end tip, gripped his collar, and he

started to hop on the spot while counting backwards.

The gentleman came running into view, waving his straw boater at them. 'That's my umbrella!' he shouted.

'Seventeen . . . sixteen . . . fifteen . . .'

Pernickety Boo and Sylvie Moonshine opened their eyes and looked around. They were back under the horse chestnut tree, and Mum and Georgie were in the kitchen, exactly where they'd left them.

'That was close,' said Sylvie Moonshine.

'Time travel,' said Pernickety Boo, 'is not all it's cracked up to be.'

Sylvie Moonshine laughed. 'It's good fun though,' she said. 'When shall we do it again?'

CHAPTER

18

An invitation arrived for Sylvie Moonshine. Her friend Maude was having a fancy-dress party for her birthday. There were to be games, a magician and an enormous cake.

There wouldn't be time to go time travelling again until after the party. Granny was making Sylvie Moonshine a new dress especially for the occasion, and she needed Sylvie Moonshine for fittings. Sylvie Moonshine wanted to look just like the little girl she had seen at the umbrella parade. Granny found a picture of a costume matching Sylvie

Moonshine's description in one of her books.

'I can copy this,' she said. 'It's from the Edwardian era – that was long ago.'

'Perhaps we can go back to the Edwardian era,' said Sylvie Moonshine from her bed the night before the party.

'I'd been hoping to see elephants,' said Pernickety Boo from his bed. 'If we'd stayed a bit longer, they might have turned up.'

He was wondering when he'd find another glove to eat. It had been a few days since he'd had a good nibble of a finger or thumb. Sylvie Moonshine fell asleep, but hours later he was lying in his little bed, still wide awake, thinking how hungry he was.

The clock in the kitchen chimed midnight, and Jimjam loped into the bedroom with what looked like a dead bird in his mouth.

'What's that?' whispered Pernickety Boo nervously.

'A glove I dug up in the garden,' said Jimjam. 'I shook the dirt off it.'

Pernickety Boo climbed out of bed.

'I thought you looked like you'd lost your whiz,' said Jimjam. 'I've another one for you downstairs, and my lady friend would like to say hello. But please, whatever you do, don't mention Doris and her Amazing Cats. It wouldn't do my street cred any good if it got around.'

By the time Pernickety Boo had eaten the glove and hopped downstairs, he was already feeling much more like himself. In the kitchen was a cat whose name, Jimjam said, was Lilypot.

'Hello,' she purred.

Her fur was creamy, her tail, ears and face were chocolatey, and her eyes were very, very blue. Pernickety Boo thought she was beautiful.

But when he told her about the birthday party he and Sylvie Moonshine were going to that day, she said, 'I wouldn't.'

'You wouldn't what?' asked Pernickety Boo, starting to nibble on the other glove Jimjam had found for him.

'I wouldn't go if I were you,' she said.

'Why not?'

Lilypot's eyes seemed to become larger, and Pernickety Boo felt he was being drawn into their blue depths.

'Forgetfulness,' she said. 'And now I must leave or I'll be missed.'

'Beautiful, isn't she?' said Jimjam after he'd seen his lady friend home.

Pernickety Boo was on the point of saying she reminded him of a designer handbag he once knew, but thought better of it.

'What did Lilypot mean by "forgetfulness"?' he asked.

'Search my litter tray,' said Jimjam. He yawned. 'Now, my old brolly, if you'll excuse me, I need a catnap.'

As Pernickety Boo was on his way back to bed, he saw a box in the hall by the front door. Something about it was calling to him. He looked inside and found gloves, all neatly labelled and lying in a row. There were so many of them, a bit like the drawer of gloves in Granny's house. For a minute, perhaps only a second – a rather short second – a tiny thought came to him that this box of gloves might be important. But he was still terribly hungry, so he took some of the gloves – maybe two pairs, perhaps it was more like three, all right it was four pairs – up to bed with him.

In the morning, Georgie was in a rush to get to the film studio where she was working. She took the box of gloves and was gone before breakfast. Pernickety Boo thought nothing more about them, except he felt very full and very happy.

The party started at two o'clock and Granny was going to take them. They were about to leave when Georgie phoned for Mum. Pernickety Boo was in the hall where the telephone was, and he listened as Mum said she had no idea what happened to them. No one would steal four pairs of gloves.

Steal? thought Pernickety Boo. No, he wasn't a thief. But, then again, he supposed it could be seen as stealing.

Jimjam silently appeared beside him. 'Now you're for it,' he said.

Pernickety Boo followed him into the kitchen.

'Should I say something?' he said.

'Keep mum,' said Jimjam. 'That's what I do with fur balls. I pretend they're not mine.'

Sylvie Moonshine came down looking as pretty as a picture in a white lace dress with black tights and boots, and a big bow in her hair. At that moment, the phone rang. It was Georgie again.

'I've looked everywhere. What's happened to those gloves is nothing short of a mystery,' Mum was saying to her, and Pernickety Boo was building up to confessing he'd eaten them when Granny arrived.

'Come on,' said Granny, 'or we'll be late.'

Mum said to Sylvie Moonshine, 'Are you sure it's a good idea to take Pernickety Boo?'

'Of course it is,' said Sylvie Moonshine.

CHAPTER

19

Maude's party was full of little girls and boys wearing all sorts of fancy dress, from princesses to frogs. Her father was at the front door, collecting what he called 'dangerous items'.

'We don't want our little guests tripping up or being poked in the ribs,' he said in a jolly voice.

Sylvie Moonshine rushed off to play musical chairs while Maude's father put Pernickety Boo in a hat stand with a non-speaking, upright umbrella.

The children gathered to watch a magician. This was supposed to be the main feature of the birthday party, but the magician Maude's mother had booked had toothache and wasn't able to come. In his place, he had sent someone he didn't know very well, who worked in a magic shop near Embankment Station in London.

This man had large whiskers, a cape and a top hat that was too big for him. He looked nervous when he saw how many little children there were. He stood behind a table covered in a cloth of gold stars.

'For my first trick,' he said, 'I will fill these cups from this jug of plain tap water.' With a shaky hand, he built a sort of pyramid out of paper cups. 'The water in each cup will turn a different colour.'

He poured water into each cup, and in each one it changed colour. So far so good – until the pyramid collapsed and made a terrible mess on the cream carpet.

'Whoops-a-daisy . . .' said the magician.

Maude's parents hurried to the kitchen to fetch paper towels while coloured liquid oozed into their brand-new carpet.

The magician's next trick didn't go down any better. He tried to guess the name of the birthday girl.

'Mabel,' he said triumphantly.

Maude stood up. 'You're a hopeless magician,' she said. 'My name is Maude.'

'Darling, don't be rude,' said Maude's mum.

'Wait,' said the magician. He removed his top hat and waved his wand over it. 'I will make Mabel – I mean Maude – a birthday cake.'

Pernickety Boo, propped up in the hat stand, was having a pleasant dream about elephants until he dreamed he heard a voice he recognised. A voice that filled him with dread. He woke up with a start, unable to tell if the voice had been real or if he'd imagined it. He listened for sounds coming from the party. All was quiet.

The children were silent, watching open-mouthed as the magician broke six eggs into his top hat. Then he added flour, sugar, milk and butter and whisked his wand over it all.

'Abracadabra,' he said, then peered into his hat. 'Well, where has it gone?'

He turned his hat upside down, and nothing came out.

'That's good,' said Maude, laughing. 'Where's the cake?'

Even the magician looked a little surprised. He put the hat on his head and the eggs, flour, sugar, milk and butter ran down his face. Everyone fell about laughing except the magician, who had to take a break to clean himself up.

Pernickety Boo saw him dash into the hall and up the stairs. Even covered in cake mixture, Pernickety Boo would have recognised those grey whiskers anywhere.

The magician was none other than Pernickety Boo's sorcerer.

There wasn't a moment to waste, and Pernickety Boo had just climbed out of the hat stand when the front doorbell rang. Maude's father opened the door.

'Stephen – there you are,' he said. 'This is a desperate situation.'

'It's raining again,' said the man at the door, putting both his umbrella and Pernickety Boo in the hat stand.

'Uncle Stephen!' shouted Maude, running up to him. 'We have the worst magician. He's ruined Mum's new carpet AND he got my name wrong.'

'There'll be a riot if the children aren't entertained,' Maude's father said, just as the sorcerer came down the stairs.

'Leave it to me,' said Uncle Stephen. 'I know a few magic tricks.'

Maude led him to the sitting room, and immediately he had all the children entranced.

'Well, I never,' said the sorcerer. 'I was only doing this as a favour. It's not my fault my spells have gone wrong. Boohoo.'

'Thank you for coming,' said Maude's father, opening the front door.

Pernickety Boo sighed with relief as he watched the sorcerer leave. But to his horror the man turned round and came back before Maude's father had closed the door.

'I nearly forgot my umbrella,' the sorcerer said, and lifted Pernickety Boo from the hat stand, gripping him tightly round his snout. 'I'd lose my head if it wasn't screwed on. Ha ha!'

Panic flooded Pernickety Boo. He had woken up from

a dream into a nightmare. The sorcerer opened Pernickety Boo's canopy, and now he was going down the garden path, along the pavement, away from Maude's house and, worst of all, away from Sylvie Moonshine.

What to do? thought Pernickety Boo. *What to do?*

At Turnbury Station, the sorcerer boarded a train and sat down, muttering to himself for the entire journey while resting his hands on the top of Pernickety Boo's head.

As much as Pernickety Boo wanted to say, 'Take me back,' he knew that if he spoke he might never, ever see Sylvie Moonshine again. He felt an odd sensation – one he hadn't felt before. A tear rolled down his snout and fell onto the shoe of the sorcerer, who didn't notice.

When they got off the train, the sorcerer fought his way through the other passengers at the busy station. People were rushing and pushing and shoving.

'Out of my way,' said the sorcerer, using Pernickety Boo to part the crowd.

Down the escalator they went and along a tunnel, until they came to the Circle Line.

'That's the last time I try to help out a friend,' muttered the sorcerer as the Circle Line train drew up and they got on.

He propped Pernickety Boo against the seat while he searched in his pockets for his ticket.

'Ah, my stop,' said the sorcerer a little later, standing up.

Pernickety Boo wondered, if he jumped, whether he might be able to travel back in time to Sylvie Moonshine. He jumped once, he jumped twice, but all that happened was he found himself going down the escalator and to the Circle Line again.

'That's the last time I try to help out a friend,' muttered the sorcerer, getting on the train.

Pernickety Boo had another go at jumping, but he found it hard to jump on the spot with the train rattling along.

And it occurred to him that even if he did travel back to when he was with Sylvie Moonshine, what happened next would be the same as before, with the same result.

Exhausted and defeated, Pernickety Boo watched as the sorcerer left the tube train without him, the doors sliding shut between them. And it was then that Pernickety Boo knew he was abandoned, forgotten and lost.

CHAPTER

20

Once more, Pernickety Boo found himself in the Lost Property Office at Baker Street with a label tied round his collar. It had no name on it, only the time and place he was handed in:

Five thirty, the Circle Line at Gloucester Road Station.

Once more, he was put on one of the green metal racks along with all the other lost and forgotten umbrellas. And for the first time he felt his magical powers drain away from him. He felt himself to be nothing more than an ordinary, unloved umbrella – one of the thousands abandoned every year. Gone was his comfortable bed, gone his postcard of Jumbo, gone his beloved owner, Sylvie Moonshine.

There would be no more sunshine switch; no more Jimjam to keep him company. No more Mum and Georgie. Just the endless strip light that was switched on in the morning and off in the evening. Just the vague whiff of damp that hung about the place from so many unshed tears.

What was he to do? Pernickety Boo felt hopeless, and was sure he'd been there for weeks and weeks already. Time was nothing more than a fur ball. He didn't want to talk to anyone. At first he'd hoped Sylvie Moonshine would find him, but then a heavy thought came to him, rattling the ribs of his conscience. Perhaps Georgie and Mum had decided they didn't want a glove thief living in their house. Perhaps he'd been seen as setting a bad example to Sylvie Moonshine. How he regretted not owning up to eating gloves in the first place, when Mum had asked what he liked for breakfast.

'Back again?' said the bowed walking stick, hopping up to him. 'What happened this time?'

178

'I don't want to talk about it,' said Pernickety Boo. 'It's too painful.'

'I felt a lot like you when I first came here,' said the bowed walking stick. 'I was unable to express my feelings until you helped me talk. Since then, I've been more upright in my outlook on life, and I've understood something important.'

'What's that?' asked Pernickety Boo gloomily.

'That I was bowed for a reason.'

Pernickety Boo closed his eyes.

'Don't you want to know the reason?' said the walking stick.

'No,' said Pernickety Boo. 'I'm sorry, but I don't.'

'This isn't like you,' said the walking stick. 'You who speak four foreign languages and come from *The Time Traveller's Book of Spells*.'

'All right then,' said Pernickety Boo. 'What is the reason?'

'I was once loved, and was trusted to keep a gentleman upright, which is quite something when you think about it,' said the bowed walking stick.

Pernickety Boo rolled over and a tear ran down his snout.

'I've told all the umbrellas and walking sticks about you,' said the walking stick. 'And that you might help them hop and talk because, without you, they can't say a word.'

'I don't think I have the sparks in me any more,' said Pernickety Boo. 'That's what happens when you lose your beloved owner.'

That night he woke up in the darkness. The bowed walking stick was hopping towards his rack.

'I've brought you a glove,' he said. 'I had to push it across the floor, so it's rather dusty. But it looks tasty – if gloves are your thing.'

'I've gone off gloves,' said Pernickety Boo.

Nevertheless he sat up and nibbled it. And he sneezed. And he sneezed and sneezed over and over again.

'That's done the trick,' said the walking stick. 'All that was needed was some magic sparks.'

Looking into the night gloom of the Lost Property Office, Pernickety Boo saw all the umbrellas and walking

 180

sticks climb down from their racks and, shyly at first, hop towards him.

'You're the famous Pernickety Boo,' a lady's umbrella said.

'I'm not famous,' said Pernickety Boo.

'Yes, you are,' said a folding umbrella, who had only just been brought in. 'Look – there's a picture of you in the newspaper.'

There it was, along with a notice.

A most extraordinary umbrella, Pernickety Boo,
belonging to Sylvie Moonshine, is missing. It was last seen
at Maude Brownfield's birthday party in Turnbury.

A reward of £100 is offered.

The photo was the one Georgie took of Sylvie Moonshine
and Pernickety Boo before they time travelled to the umbrella
parade.

'It shows you're wanted,' said a parasol. 'And maybe we
all are.'

'Yes, all of us,' said the umbrellas and walking sticks together.

This cheered up Pernickety Boo, and he said he was
sure that owners with non-wobbly heads were looking for
them too.

He kept the newspaper and helped himself to a few gloves.
That night there was quite a party; the umbrellas showed off
their different canopies, even the ones with the broken ribs,
while the walking sticks compared ferrules.

The following morning, when the staff came into work,
they couldn't think who had left the lights on.

Pernickety Boo read and reread the piece in the newspaper. He kept it neatly folded in his canopy, and only when no one was about did he take it out and look at it again. Sylvie Moonshine hadn't given up on him, and £100 was a lot of money.

It was the time of the annual clear-out at the Lost Property Office: the day when those items that had been left there a long time were sold or given away or, worse still, dumped. The bowed walking stick had been taken from his rack and, together with a group of sorry-looking sticks, put in a bin labelled DUMP.

'Well, I suppose I'll be gone tomorrow,' said the bowed walking stick. 'It's been nice knowing you, Pernickety Boo, and I hope your owner finds you. Can you read what's written on this container I'm in?'

Pernickety Boo couldn't bring himself to say it. Instead, he said, 'Antique.'

'That's good,' said the walking stick.

This is now a rescue mission, thought Pernickety Boo.

He gathered together all the other umbrellas and sticks to help. They only had to wait for the Lost Property Office to shut, then they would put Pernickety Boo's plan into action.

The office was about to close when a man walked in. Pernickety Boo overheard what he was saying.

'Yes,' he said, 'a somewhat bowed walking stick. I lost it years ago, shortly before I went travelling. It's a family heirloom, and it belonged to my ancestor. The story is that he used it all the time after he lost his leg at Waterloo. No, the battle, not the station.'

'That's my owner,' said the bowed walking stick. 'I would know his voice anywhere. But how will the Lost Property Office assistant know it's me he wants? My label has gone.'

All the umbrellas and walking sticks stood to attention.

'Change of plan,' said Pernickety Boo, and breathed sparks at a suitcase. The suitcase had wheels and quickly rolled itself into position.

Pernickety Boo helped the bowed walking stick out of

the bin. With some effort, the walking stick succeeded – at the third attempt – in hopping onto the suitcase.

The Lost Property Office assistant was saying, 'Usually, we don't keep anything that long, sir.'

Meanwhile, remembering the light that followed him at the circus, Pernickety Boo found a torch and, balancing it on a rack, he now switched it on, pointing the beam at the suitcase.

'But wait,' said the man. 'There behind you – look.'

'There's nothing behind me, sir, but racks of lost property,' said the Lost Property Office assistant.

'No – look! It's my walking stick!'

And there, standing on the suitcase in the pool of light, was the bowed walking stick.

'Well, fancy that,' said the assistant.

'That's my old walking stick,' said the man. 'After all these years, that's my dear friend.'

The assistant scratched his head. 'Sometimes,' he said, 'I get the feeling something funny is going on here.'

Pernickety Boo turned off the torch and watched as the bowed walking stick disappeared into the sunshine of a Truly Loved smile.

It's no good feeling sorry for myself, thought Pernickety Boo. Nothing good will come of it.

He had to believe Sylvie Moonshine would find him, just as she'd believed that he would rescue her when she was chained up in Billy Turpin's treehouse. Yes, looking on the bright side gave you hope.

CHAPTER
21

Sylvie Moonshine was heartbroken. Three weeks had passed, and Mum and Georgie had done everything possible to find Pernickety Boo. Georgie had tracked down the sorcerer to the magic shop at Embankment, but he couldn't remember taking an umbrella from the Brownfields' house.

'I went there and back by train . . . No, I didn't have an umbrella. I'm absolutely certain about that. I didn't arrive with one so why would you think I left with one?'

'Because,' said Georgie, 'Mr Brownfield saw you take one from the hat stand.'

'It must have been my one successful magical illusion,' said the sorcerer. 'No, madam, I had no umbrella.'

Mum went to Turnbury Station where there was a basket full of lost items, but not an umbrella among them.

It was as if Pernickety Boo had vanished into thin air.

'Perhaps he went time travelling,' said Georgie.

'But he wouldn't just disappear,' said Sylvie Moonshine flatly. 'I know that. Anyway, he told me his magic would disappear without me.'

To which Mum and Georgie could think of nothing to say. They put an advert in the local newspaper with a picture of Pernickety Boo and Sylvie and offered a reward of £100. They didn't know what more they could do.

Sylvie Moonshine didn't want to play alone in her room and took to moping in front of the TV with Jimjam.

'Do you think Jimjam's ill?' said Mum to Georgie. 'He's off his food and doesn't go out much.'

'I think he's like all of us – he's missing Pernickety Boo,' said Georgie.

Sylvie was waking up in tears in the middle of

the night, saying she was as sure as sure is certain that Pernickety Boo was calling to her.

When there was no response to the advert, a general gloom settled over the family.

'Who would have thought that the loss of an umbrella could have such a sad effect on everyone?' said Georgie.

It was a Saturday morning, and she and Mum were trying to think how to cheer up Sylvie Moonshine when Granny arrived while they were eating breakfast.

'I thought we could go to the zoo,' she said, taking off her gloves. 'We could see the elephants.'

For a moment – just a small moment – Sylvie Moonshine's face brightened. But then, 'No, Granny,' she said with a sigh. 'It's best I stay here in case Pernickety Boo turns up.'

'That's not a good idea,' said Granny firmly. 'Come on, Sylvie Moonshine. Put on your fairy wings and your clown hat, and let's catch a train to London.'

'London?' said Sylvie Moonshine.

189

'Where else would we find London Zoo?' said Granny, laughing.

That was something that even a sad girl who had lost her best brolly couldn't say no to.

When they arrived at Charing Cross Station, Granny said, 'You know, Baker Street is on the way to London Zoo.'

Sylvie Moonshine's eyes lit up. 'You mean the Lost Property Office?'

'I do indeed.'

'Oh, but it's no good, Granny,' said Sylvie Moonshine, downcast again. 'Georgie phoned them, and the man said he'd never heard of anything as daft as an umbrella that could bend in the middle – and as for opening its mouth and speaking, he didn't think that was possible.'

'He might not necessarily have known if they had Pernickety Boo,' said Granny, 'but perhaps the other people who work there will.'

'Perhaps,' said Sylvie Moonshine, and she remembered

Pernickety Boo talking about the Skeleton Staff.

That same Saturday, while Granny and Sylvie Moonshine were on the train to London, the sorcerer was busy doing his weekend chores. Looking in the cupboard under the stairs for a scrubbing brush, he found his cauldron and remembered the last time he'd used it. He'd been trying to cast a spell from *The Time Traveller's Book of Spells*, and he'd had nothing to stir the cauldron with except a cheap, non-folding umbrella.

One thought led to another, and it was while he was cleaning the shower – something he hadn't done for ages and ages – that it came to him that he had taken an umbrella from that awful children's party. It was a handsome umbrella with a handle shaped like a dog's head. He must have left it on the tube. He stopped doing the housework, put on his hat and went to catch the train to Baker Street.

He arrived at the Lost Property Office half an hour before Sylvie Moonshine and Granny.

'Yes?' said the Lost Property Office assistant. 'How can I help?'

'My dear man,' said the sorcerer, 'I left my umbrella on the tube train. It's a non-folding umbrella with a dog's-head handle.'

The assistant was a young man who hadn't worked at the Lost Property Office for very long.

'Do you remember when you lost it?'

The sorcerer did.

'Yes,' said the assistant. 'I think we might have it. It was handed in at Gloucester Road Station.'

'That will be the very one,' said the sorcerer.

The second that Pernickety Boo heard the sorcerer's voice, he knew he had to hide. If the sorcerer claimed him, the possibility of Sylvie Moonshine ever finding him was even less than zero. He wriggled and hopped out of his rack – but where to go? Then he saw the door to the broom cupboard was open, and quickly he hid himself inside.

The assistant, walking past the broom cupboard, closed the door and locked it.

'That door should not be left open – it's a hazard,' he said

192

to no one in particular as he walked up and down the rows of green metal racks until he saw the label he was looking for. It was on the floor with no umbrella attached to it.

He scratched his head, feeling in a bit of a muddle. He went back to the sorcerer.

'What kind of dog's-head handle does your umbrella have?'

'Oh, you know,' said the sorcerer vaguely, 'the kind of dog's head that goes on an umbrella handle.'

The assistant went back and looked again. All he could find was a child's spotted umbrella with a Dalmatian's head for a handle. It was in a pile marked for a jumble sale.

'Come on!' called the sorcerer. 'I haven't all day.'

The assistant tied the label round the Dalmatian umbrella.

'Is this it?' he asked.

'That's it,' said the sorcerer. 'And now I'm in need of an ice cream.'

'Would you please write down your name and address?' said the assistant. But the sorcerer, without a 'good day' or a 'thank you', had gone.

193

Meanwhile, Granny and Sylvie Moonshine had taken the tube train to Baker Street.

The Lost Property Office didn't look like Sylvie Moonshine thought it would. In the window was a display of interesting things that had never been collected – a top hat, reels of films in cans, an old-fashioned camera and a stuffed alligator.

Inside, Granny asked the assistant if an umbrella with a dog's-head handle had been handed in.

'That's a coincidence,' said the assistant. 'There was a gentleman in here half an hour ago with the very same enquiry. I showed him the only one we had, and he claimed it was his.'

Sylvie Moonshine felt a horrible sick feeling in her tummy.

'Did he have big grey whiskers?'

'Yes, he did as a matter of fact.'

'It's the magician from Maude's party,' whispered Sylvie Moonshine to Granny. 'He's taken Pernickety Boo.'

'Do you have an address for this individual?' asked Granny.

'No, he left without filling in the form.'

The assistant felt sorry for Sylvie Moonshine, who he could see was on the verge of tears.

'That umbrella had a spotty Dalmatian dog's head,' he said. 'Was it yours?'

'No,' said Sylvie Moonshine, brightening. 'Mine has a purply black greyhound's head. And he can bend in the middle, sit down and use his rib tips as fingers.'

'What a charming little girl,' said the assistant, relieved that he hadn't given the whiskery gentleman the wrong umbrella. 'Such imagination.'

Sylvie Moonshine suddenly had a funny, fuzzy feeling that Pernickety Boo was in the Lost Property Office somewhere.

There was only one thing to do. She shouted as loud as she could, 'PERNICKETY BOO, WHERE ARE YOU?'

Granny and the assistant stopped talking.

'She has a loud voice for such a little girl,' said the assistant.

Granny looked at Sylvie Moonshine, and they waited. Nothing.

But Sylvie Moonshine was not to be put off. She shouted

again. 'PERNICKETY BOO, I LOVE YOU!'

The assistant, talking to Sylvie Moonshine in the way grown-ups often do when they've forgotten that once they too were small, said, 'I don't think there's an umbrella that can . . .'

'It's no good, Sylvie Moonshine,' said Granny, taking her hand. 'Let's go to the zoo.'

'Wait,' said Sylvie Moonshine. 'Listen, do you hear that? It's the sound Pernickety Boo's sparks make.'

'Is it?' said Granny.

The assistant smiled. 'It's the broom cupboard,' he said. 'Something wrong with the lock, I believe.'

'Excuse me,' said a polite voice behind him.

The assistant spun round and could see no one – nothing except for an umbrella where an umbrella shouldn't be.

'Would you please let me through?' said Pernickety Boo, trying to appear calm, which he was finding tricky. 'That's my owner, you see.'

The speechless assistant lifted the countertop and watched open-mouthed as Pernickety Boo hopped out and wrapped Sylvie Moonshine in his canopy.

'Oh, Pernickety Boo, I have missed you,' said Sylvie Moonshine, kissing the top of his greyhound head. 'And so have Mum and Georgie and Jimjam.'

'I've missed you too. I was so worried you might not find me,' said Pernickety Boo.

'I would have kept looking for you until I was a hundred and five,' said Sylvie Moonshine.

'Does it work on batteries?' asked the assistant.

'No,' said Granny, 'it works on love.'

Never had an umbrella with a greyhound's-head handle and a small person in fairy wings and a clown hat been so pleased to see one another. They hopped and skipped all the way to London Zoo.

'This is the best of days,' said Sylvie Moonshine as they stood together, watching the elephants.

'It is,' said Pernickety Boo. He paused for a moment. 'Elephants are much, much bigger than I expected.'

'I don't think you would have been very good at looking after them,' said Sylvie Moonshine.

'No. I dreamed of elephants, but there was only one owner for me, and that was you, Sylvie Moonshine.'

The three of them had their picnic lunch in Regent's Park.

'Was it the sorcerer who took you from the party?' asked Granny.

'Yes,' said Pernickety Boo. 'He's very forgetful.'

He couldn't help but notice that Granny was taking from her handbag a pair of mouthwatering suede gloves.

'I think this is what you like to eat, Pernickety Boo,' said Granny with a twinkle in her eye.

'I do,' said Pernickety Boo. 'I should have said so when I first arrived at Sylvie Moonshine's house, but I felt . . . I felt . . .'

'Embarrassed?' suggested Granny.

'Yes, that was it,' said Pernickety Boo. 'Embarrassed.'

After their picnic lunch, they decided all they wanted to do was go home to 3 Rose Terrace and see Georgie and Mum.

But Granny had one more surprise for Sylvie Moonshine. 'When I was young,' she said, 'the best treat of all was a ride in a black London taxi.'

'Wow!' said Sylvie Moonshine as a black cab drew up at the park gates.

'Where to?' said the taxi driver.

'Charing Cross Station, please,' said Granny as they all climbed in.

Pernickety Boo sat next to Sylvie Moonshine. She had her hand round his collar, and a warm feeling ran through him. He was back again with his beloved owner.

'I'm going to make you an umbrella carrier,' said Granny to Sylvie Moonshine. 'You can wear it strapped to you so you won't ever lose Pernickety Boo again.'

'That's a very good idea, Granny,' said Pernickety Boo.

'Did that bumbershoot just talk?' said the taxi driver.

'That what?' said Sylvie Moonshine.

'Bumbershoot,' said the taxi driver. 'It's an old-fashioned word for umbrella. I've never seen an umbrella that can talk and bend in the middle. It must be a proper bumbershoot.'

'I'm not a bumbershoot,' said Pernickety Boo. 'I'm a

finickety, pernickety, time-travelling umbrella.'

The taxi driver burst out laughing. 'That's a first,' he said.

They arrived home at teatime. Mum had made a cake and laid the table with an embroidered tablecloth. She and Georgie hoped Sylvie Moonshine might be a bit more cheerful after her visit to the zoo.

The front door burst open and charging into the living room came the happiest Sylvie Moonshine they'd seen in ages.

'Look!' she shouted. 'Look who's with me!'

Pernickety Boo knew by the welcome he received that he was truly home. It was clear to him as soon as the family sat down for tea. He just listened as everyone started talking at once, and Granny and Sylvie Moonshine told the mums how they had rescued Pernickety Boo from the Lost Property Office. And about their visit to the elephants at London Zoo, and their picnic and the taxi ride to Charing Cross Station.

Mum served Pernickety Boo with a plate of one delicious

green glove and one mouthwatering red one.

She said, 'We were a bit slow about the gloves. But we'd never met a Pernickety Boo before and had no idea what one ate.'

'I thought you wouldn't want me once you knew I'd taken the gloves,' said Pernickety Boo. 'And I was afraid you were worried about Sylvie Moonshine and me time travelling.'

'I just wish I'd had a Pernickety Boo to time travel with when I was small,' said Georgie.

At that moment, there was a rumble of thunder, and Jimjam hurtled through the catflap and jumped onto the chair beside Pernickety Boo.

'Glad to have you back, you daft brolly,' he said to Pernickety Boo, rubbing his head against him and purring. 'I was surprised to find I missed you. The sunshine switch is still playing up.' He sniffed. 'Oh, excuse me, I smell sardines for tea. Now that's a treat.' And off he went to his bowl.

Pernickety Boo looked round the table at the happy faces. 'I always wanted to belong to someone, to mean something to someone,' he said. 'Now I have a family, and I know I do belong. Which, when you think about it, is quite an achievement for a well-educated umbrella from *The Time Traveller's Book of Spells*.'

Sylvie Moonshine smiled at him, and he felt himself to be bathed in the sunshine of the Truly Loved.

THE END